THE EDINBURGH MURDERS

DI GILES BOOK 14

ANNA-MARIE MORGAN

ALSO BY ANNA-MARIE MORGAN

In the DI Giles Series:

Book 1 - Death Master

Book 2 - You Will Die

Book 3 - Total Wipeout

Book 4 - Deep Cut

Book 5 - The Pusher

Book 6 - Gone

Book 7 - Bone Dancer

Book 8 - Blood Lost

Book 9 - Angel of Death

Book 10 - Death in the Air

Book 11 - Death in the Mist

Book 12 - Death under Hypnosis

Book 13 - Fatal Turn

Copyright © 2020 by Anna-Marie Morgan

All rights reserved.

No part of this book may be reproduced in any form or by any electronic or mechanical means, including information storage and retrieval systems, without written permission from the author, except for the use of brief quotations in a book review.

For Jean,
Thank you for being who you are, and for lighting up my world

1

MURDER IN REID'S CLOSE

Trevor Macpherson tossed the stubbed-out cigarette into the putrid trash spilling over from a faded dumpster. Clouds of beer-soaked breath reflected the light from a nearby streetlamp.

Turning up his collar against the late October wind, the ex-detective turned from the door and into Reid's Close, the lane that would take him through Holyrood, at the back of the Scottish parliament, and on to St Margaret's Loch, where he had left his BMW.

He couldn't walk straight. Persuaded by his friends to stay on at Jack Hendry's sixtieth birthday party, he had drunk far more than planned. With Covid entering its second wave, another lockdown could happen any day. This was their last get-together for a while. It was not a hard sell. Besides, he needed information, and this might be the last time he would shine his light in the darkest corners. Alcohol loosened tongues better than anything he knew.

He had known most of those at the gathering since their school days in the city of his birth. Edinburgh was home, and though London had housed and employed him for the previous thirty-five years, it was to Scotland he would always return.

Now retired, he intended seeing out the rest of his days there. To him, there was no better place.

A tin can rattled down the alley. He swung round, heart thumping, knowing his nerves were ridiculous. The alley was empty. A coronavirus pandemic had seen to that.

A dark shape passed to his right.

Macpherson stumbled into the wall, his shoulder taking the impact. "Christ!" He hauled himself up, rubbing his injured arm, eyes scouring the corridor's light and shadowed places. He saw nothing. The alley was silent.

Straightening his overcoat, he turned his attention to locating the car fob in its pockets. Not that Mack intended driving, he needed his overnight bag from the boot.

A black-clad figure in a skeleton-jawed face mask jumped out in front of him. In the intruder's right hand, a terrifying monster of a knife, its serrated edge glinting in the streetlight.

The retired detective gasped, holding up his hands, palms outward. "Listen..." His voice trembled. Sweat formed nuggets on his brow. "I- I don't want any trouble."

The hooded figure threw the weapon hand-to-hand. The air was thick with menace.

Macpherson's alcohol-hampered mind struggled for a way out. Perhaps he could take the assailant by surprise. His gaze dropped to the blade. A chill thickened his blood as the figure thrust it at him.

He stepped back, terror clarifying beer-addled thought, hands remaining outwards at the man in black. "What do you want? I have money." He pulled out his wallet, opening it to tempt the would-be attacker. A restaurant receipt tumbled to the floor. "How much do you want?"

The figure took a step towards him, knife extended.

Macpherson threw the wallet to the ground, as they had trained him to do, creating dissonance in the assailant's mind. If he went for the prize, the ex-detective would make his move.

He swallowed hard when, having glanced at the currency in the road, the man returned his hawkish, unblinking eyes to the detective. Money was not the aim. This wasn't robbery.

Macpherson ran, aiming for the tunnel at the end of the close, at the back of Holyrood.

It took moments to end a life. That, and several deep stabs and slashes with the blade.

The killer stayed to watch his victim's chest move less with every inhalation until obvious breathing ceased. He wiped the knife on the detective's jacket while the latter lay still and silent. Serrated teeth tore into the fabric.

The killer opened the zip on his trousers, urinating on the dying man before taking off down the alley.

A light breeze fluttered the loose receipt. The open wallet lay where it had fallen, next to the stricken Macpherson. The last tiny cloud of beer-sodden breath dissipated.

"It's a no, isn't it?" Tasha tilted her head, her eyes searching Yvonne's face, worry creasing her forehead.

Behind them, the fire crackled in the grate, its light dancing on the psychologist's chocolate hair.

The DI sighed, running a hand through her blonde, mussed mop. "It's not no."

"Is it yes?"

"I don't know..."

"Have you thought it over at all?" Tasha's frown deepened.

"Of course I have. I know I said six weeks-"

"What's stopping you, Yvonne? What are the barriers? Talk to me... Please?" The psychologist's gaze softened as she placed a hand on her partner's shoulder. "Are you unsure about us?"

"It's not that..."

"Then what?" Tasha picked up her glass of brandy from the hearth, swirling it around as she leaned back on the floor cushions in front of the fire.

A hot ember spat onto the rug.

Yvonne hopped up, tossing it back into the flames, rubbing at the blackened patch left behind with her fingers. "I'm still not out to everyone, Tasha. You know that. Some people don't even know we are living together."

"Does that matter?" Tasha asked, her voice almost a whisper.

The DI shrugged. "I don't know. It shouldn't, I realise that."

"Do you need more time? I'm not trying to rush you."

Yvonne closed her hand over her partner's. "Perhaps, a little longer, Tasha, just until I get my act together."

The psychologist nodded, red-rimmed eyes glistening; lips pressed tight together. "I love you," she whispered. "Take all the time you need."

"I love-"

Tasha's mobile vibrated on the coffee table. "Oh, hell..." She jumped up. "Who's ringing me now?"

The DI scratched her head, concern over letting her partner down knotted her stomach.

"It's the Met," the psychologist frowned at the phone, clearing her throat. "Tasha Phillips. What? What do you mean? Dead? Murdered? How? Why?" She sat, placing a hand to her temple.

After several minutes, Tasha ended the call, confusion in her glazed eyes.

Yvonne rose from her seat to stand next to her partner."Tasha?"

"I don't believe it. Mack is dead..." She shook her head. "Mack is dead."

"Who's Mack?" The DI put a hand on her arm, turning Tasha to face her. "Talk to me, love."

"Trevor. Trevor Macpherson. One of my oldest friends. He retired from the Metropolitan Police last year."

"What's happened?"

"He's been murdered in an alleyway in Edinburgh." She raised wide eyes to the DI. "They cut him up and left him in the road."

"Oh, heavens." Yvonne put an arm around the psychologist's shoulders. "Tasha, I'm so sorry."

"I spoke to him only a couple of weeks ago. He said he was living the dream; enjoying his retirement. I can't believe..." The psychologist's voice trailed away, her eyes staring into space.

"Do they know who did it?"

Tasha shook her head. "I don't think so. Edinburgh MIT has launched a murder inquiry. I have to find out if I can help?"

The DI pursed her lips. "That probably won't be possible, Tasha, at least not officially. They would consider you too close to the case."

"I can't stand by, Yvonne, I need to do something. "

"Has he got a family?"

The psychologist shrugged. "His wife divorced him years ago. She lives somewhere in London. They chose not to have children. I think he regretted that in later life." She ran her hands through her hair. "Who on earth would want to murder Mack?"

"Perhaps it was a random attack? But he will, most likely, have collected a few enemies during a lifetime as a detective, Tasha. Criminals have long memories. How long had you known him?"

"Oh God," Tasha frowned. "Let's see... Best part of fifteen years, I'd say. I met him when I was twenty-four. He got me my first job with the Met after I qualified with my doctorate. I was so naïve back then. He gave me one heck of a grounding in police work, helped me put what I'd learned into practice, hunting down some of the worst serial offenders in the country. Mack had an enormous influence on many of us. The man was a larger-than-life character in the force. He was one of the best, Yvonne. One from the old mould. Took no messing. Hard when needed, but soft as marshmallows on the inside. Mack saw straight through situations and people, not unlike yourself."

"I see."

"I can't believe he's gone. You know, even after he retired, he would still phone us to find out how things were going. And we knew we could contact him anytime if we needed his advice. He'll leave a big hole in many people's lives."

"I'm sorry." The DI pulled her partner into her arms. "It's a shock, Tasha. Come and sit down. I'll make you a cup of tea."

"I want to go there."

"Where? London?"

"No, Edinburgh. I want to see for myself where he died. Even if they refuse my help."

Yvonne nodded. "Of course, I understand."

Tasha clung to her, sinking into the DI's soft empathy.

Yvonne swayed her gently. "They'll get him, my love. Trust me, I am sure they will find and punish his killer. Murder is the toughest crime to get away with."

2

HARD ACT TO SWALLOW

Yvonne loaded her supermarket shop into the car boot, cursing as she arranged and rearranged the bags so the lid would close.

Tasha had left for Edinburgh five days before, since which time they had spoken by video call only once. The DI missed her. She hoped the psychologist would get the closure she craved and be able to make sense of her friend's loss.

She was still pondering events when her phone rang.

It was an unknown number.

"Yvonne Giles." She put a finger in the opposite ear, reducing the traffic noise.

"Yvonne, it's Tasha. I'm phoning from Leith Station, in Edinburgh."

"Heavens... You work fast." Yvonne opened her car door and slipped into the driver's seat. "Have you spoken to the investigation team? Have they accepted your help?"

"They haven't officially, not yet. But, the good news is, the lead investigator is DI Grant McKenzie. I know him. Well, I know a little of him."

"You do? That's great."

"It's a small world, isn't it? I prepared a profile for his team seven years ago. Mack recommended me to them. Grant McKenzie is the youngest brother of Colin McKenzie, one of Mack's friends from college."

"No way... Wow, it's a small world."

"It is. Grant has given me access to crime scene photographs, but warned me they may question Met detectives, as part of the investigation."

"Makes sense."

"I'd like you to see the photos, but I need to run it past McKenzie first. I don't want to get on the wrong side of him."

"No," Yvonne agreed. "Not if you want to stay involved in the case."

"There's something else." Tasha paused.

"Go on," Yvonne prompted.

"Grant doesn't know that Mack and I were good friends. He only knows that I helped Mack and his team by providing profiles for their investigations."

"Are you going to tell him about your friendship?" The DI frowned.

"I want to take part in the inquiry, Yvonne, prepare a profile, you know? He won't let me if he knows I was close to the victim."

"What if he finds out?"

"I'll deal with that if it happens."

"He'll know when he questions colleagues at the Met."

"Yes but, by then, I should have provided them an idea of the killer."

"McKenzie will not like you hiding it from him."

"You're repeating yourself."

Yvonne sighed. "Send me the photos and, if he's okay with that, I'll look at them and get back to you."

"Thank you, darling. I miss you."

"I miss you too. Please, do nothing daft. Speak soon." The DI clicked off the call and started the engine, disappointed that her partner wouldn't be home soon. Understanding her reasons didn't make Tasha's absence any easier to bear.

Twenty-four hours later, Yvonne was pouring over the images of the Reid's Alley crime scene, emailed to her by Tasha.

Some showed the entire body, while others were of specific injuries and blood spatter.

The dead man lay on his back, his legs drawn up in a foetal position as though he had been trying to protect himself from the knife man. He lay parallel to the alley walls. The blood, having pooled around him, had continued to stream along the alley to the drain. A blood-soaked receipt lay on the ground next to him, along with his open wallet. His only other companions were various items of litter, blown around by the wind.

Closeups showed the extent and severity of the injuries to his stomach and chest. One photo depicted a six-inch cut in the dead man's jacket, along with a smear of blood, as though the killer had cut the material while wiping the weapon.

The last photo caused her breath to catch in her throat.

She shuddered. Protruding from Trevor Macpherson's left eye was a cocktail stick. The killer had placed it precisely in the centre of the dilated pupil.

Yvonne phoned Tasha.

The psychologist answered after several rings, getting straight to the point. "Did you receive the pictures?"

"I did. The killer went to town on him, didn't he?"

Tasha sighed. "He didn't hold back, that's for sure. Mack didn't stand a chance. His blood alcohol level was eighty-two milligrams per hundred millilitres."

"He'd been drinking?"

"He was celebrating a friend's birthday, apparently."

"A police officer?"

"No, a civilian. Mack left early because of the Covid lockdown. He would bend rules occasionally, but rarely ever break them. He was a good man."

"The birthday drinks... Did they involve party food at all?"

"Are you thinking of the cocktail stick in his eye?"

"Yes."

"I wondered that, too. However, I'm told there was were no cocktail sticks at the gathering. It's one of the first things uniformed officers asked the friends. It was a small get-together, and they only had alcohol, crisps, and nuts. It was in a hotel room. One of Mack's friends was travelling from Glasgow and had booked an overnight stay. They held the gathering there."

"I see."

"I'd love you to be here with me, Yvonne."

"I would love to be there, Tasha. I miss you, but you know I cannot drop everything."

"I do." Tasha sighed. "I have to go, I'm sorry. I'll call you tonight."

The DI closed the crime scene photos on her laptop, pondering the circumstances of Mack's death.

She checked her watch. Midday. The DCI hadn't been out of his office since his arrival at just before nine. Yvonne went to his office.

"Come in."

She cleared her throat, pushing open the door.

"Yvonne, how's it going out there?"

She took in his ordered appearance and bright eyes. He was well-rested, unlike herself. "Sir, I was wondering if I might take two weeks' leave. I-"

"Two weeks? Sure." He nodded. "Why not? When do you want them?" He crossed over to the planner on his wall.

She grimaced. "Now, please, sir."

"Now?" He frowned. "What do you mean, now? As in this minute?"

Yvonne's eyes were on the window, and the sun trying to break through the thick cloud. "Starting tomorrow would be fine, Chris."

"Tomorrow?" He pursed his lips. "I don't know, Yvonne. It's such brief notice. When you said two weeks, I didn't realise you meant right away. That's not like you. Who's going to cover? Is something wrong?"

"A situation has come up at home. Someone close to my partner died. I said I would help her sort a few things out. Personal things." She waited, breathing fast and shallow, convinced he would refuse.

"Where are you with your cases?"

"Dewi knows where we are going with those. I think he can handle things while I'm away." She chewed the inside of her cheek, wishing she had spoken to her sergeant before approaching the DCI. Dewi was unaware of her plans to take leave.

"Have you spoken to him?"

She pulled a face, her fingers entwined.

"You haven't told him, have you?" He sighed. "Look, I know you well enough to know you don't ask for last-minute leave unless you have a personal crisis on your hands. I won't press you about what the problem is, I just hope you're okay. Speak to Dewi. If you are both happy that the cases are under control, you can have leave from tomorrow."

"Thank you, sir."

"Oh and, Yvonne?"

She swallowed. "Yes?"

"I hope everything works out okay." He tilted his head. "Give Tasha my condolences."

She nodded. "I will, thank you."

3

MIST AND MURK

"What are you after?" DS Dewi Hughes laughed, putting his mug down. "I know that glint in your eye only too well."

She glanced around CID, pulling up a chair, her voice low. "I've asked to go on leave tomorrow, Dewi. I'm after a two-week break. I have somewhere I need to be."

He narrowed his eyes, leaning his head back to examine her face. "That's not like you."

"Oh, don't you start."

"I'm not criticising. I'm concerned about you."

"I'm fine, Dewi. Tasha is in Scotland."

"Is she? Wait, you guys haven't split up, have you?"

"No, nothing like that. Listen, I haven't told the DCI this, but someone murdered one of Tasha's close friends in Edinburgh. His name was Trevor Macpherson, a former detective in the Met, who retired just over a year ago."

"Murdered? Have they caught the killer?"

"No, not yet."

"Hang on, you're not going up there to get involved, are you?"

"Of course not." She frowned. "Not really. My intention is to support Tasha."

"I see. And you need me to keep things going this end..."

"I do, Dewi. I know I can trust you to keep on top of it all."

"Of course you can." He nodded. "I bet you get involved. You won't be able to help yourself."

Her smile didn't reach her eyes. "I don't know. Tasha is talking to Scottish detectives about the possibility of helping with the case. That's partly why I want to be there. I have to know what she is getting herself into. She can be hot-headed when emotional. It's something I love about her, but it also scares me."

"Pot, Kettle." Dewi grinned.

"I'll keep her grounded if I am there."

"Did you say Edinburgh?" he asked, head tilted.

"Yes, why?"

"I saw something on the news yesterday morning. A stabbing, it said, behind the Scottish parliament. They said something about the victim being a police officer."

"Retired, but yes, that sounds like him. Did they say much about it?"

Dewi shook his head. "No, that was all they said."

"It's come as a heck of a shock to her. She's all over the place."

"Well, look, you can trust me to take care of things here. I'll keep the investigations moving. Just look after yourself, and Tasha, up there in Scotland. We need you back in one piece, ma'am."

"I honestly don't think they will allow me anywhere near the investigation."

Dewi laughed, placing his hands on his hips. "I think those Scottish investigators will have to fend you off."

Yvonne's grin lit up her face, relaxing her shoulders. "You're a bugger, Dewi Hughes."

EDINBURGH BATHED in a thick pall of mist which obscured parts of the city from her gaze as she stared through the taxi window.

St Margaret's Loch lay still and silent. The vaporous veil hovered above its surface, combining with the chill in the air to give the whole a sad and eerie atmosphere, as though the place itself was telling her something bad had happened.

Yvonne shuddered.

"We're here." Tasha squeezed the DI's hand.

"Was he killed at the loch? I thought you said they murdered him in an alley?" The DI stepped out of the taxi, her eyes turning to the police tape and the black BMW being loaded onto a recovery vehicle by SOCO personnel.

"No, this was where he left his car. We think he was on his way back here when they got him. They ambushed Mack much further on towards the Royal Mile."

"I see."

"I thought we could eat lunch by the loch, and walk back along Holyrood Gait, Holyrood Road, and on into Reid's Close. That's where it happened. The walk takes between fifteen and twenty minutes. DI McKenzie thinks the killer or killers might have followed him from the loch after he parked his car here earlier that afternoon."

They walked past several vehicles with the blue thistle, the emblem of Police Scotland, proudly displayed on their bonnets. Their occupants were out talking to members of the community, people who may have seen Macpherson parking his BMW on the day of the murder, and may also have unwittingly witnessed his killer.

Her gaze strayed to the loch and the swans heading towards them through the mist in search of food. She could just make out the water's edge as it rose towards the famous promontory of Arthur's Seat, the clifftop with views over the capital city. The grass was little more than stubble on the crags and cliffs.

"It's beautiful," she mused.

"It is," Tasha agreed.

A car door clunked behind, and they turned to see a grey-suited, clean-cut male striding towards them, his long, black overcoat flapping open. He ran a hand over his dark hair.

Tasha introduced them. "DI Grant McKenzie, DI Yvonne Giles. Grant is the senior investigating officer for the inquiry."

They didn't shake hands because of the two metre social distancing rule everyone had to follow whilst the Covid pandemic raged.

Yvonne estimated Grant to be around forty years old, and six-foot-one in height.

He grinned at her. "Pleased to meet you. I've heard a lot about the famous DI Giles."

She shot Tasha a glance.

"Och, not from Doctor Phillips here." He laughed.

"Then where?" Yvonne couldn't help smiling back. "I'm surprised anyone in Scotland has heard of me."

"Jeezo, you've got a bit of a reputation, lady. You're not half-bad at catching murderers."

She grimaced, colour rising to her cheeks. "I've caught one or two." She mused that his broad and friendly Scots accent was at odds with his neat, measured appearance. She could better imagine him letting it all hang out in a t-shirt and jeans.

"Didn't you nearly get yourself killed a couple of years back?"

She pressed her lips together.

"I'm sorry." He tilted his head. "I didn't mean... Jings, that was insensitive of me."

She held up a hand. "It's okay. Yes, I did nearly get myself killed. How did you know that?"

"Och, Yvonne. Police forces talk to each other. It's a privilege to meet you. You can tag along with us for as long as you're here in Edinburgh. We'd enjoy having your perspective on things." A smile creased his eyes.

"Thank you." She grinned back. "I may take you up on that."

"You're not married?" He glanced at her left hand.

His question caught her off guard. She flicked her eyes towards Tasha and winced. "No... Not yet."

"Och, I'm not propositioning you." He held his hand up, flashing his wedding ring. "I'm happily married with three young-uns under the age of twelve. I am way too tired for hanky-panky, even if I wanted to play around, which I don't." He laughed. "No offence."

"None taken." Yvonne liked him. He spoke plainly. People would always know where they stood with him.

"He's laid back, but he knows what he is doing," Tasha whispered as the SIO wandered off to talk to the crime scene officers before they left with Mack's vehicle.

"He seems like a good man." Yvonne nodded. "So, Macpherson parked out here. Do we know what time?"

"A witness said it was just after five in the afternoon."

"And, what made MIT think the killer followed him?"

"A witness said someone with their hood up, wearing a

facemask, had been hanging around by the loch. That person followed Mack into Holyrood Gait." Tasha pointed in the direction from which they had approached in the taxi earlier. "McKenzie said the friends met around five-thirty, and Mack left just after nine that night."

"Just after nine? Was that because of the ten o'clock curfew?"

"Seems likely."

"I don't know how much use I can be, Tasha, but if I can help, I will."

"Thank you, my darling. You are already helping by being here. The rest is a bonus."

"Are you working this case officially? I mean, will you be preparing a profile for them?" The DI studied her partner's face, knowing that an answer in the affirmative would mean the psychologist being away from home for longer.

Tasha nodded. "I've offered my services to the MIT, pro bono. If it had been anyone other than Mack, I likely wouldn't have, but..." She sighed. "I have to do this."

"Hey..." The DI put her hand on Tasha's arm. "It's okay. I understand. I would do the same in your position."

"This could take weeks, Yvonne. I know you can't be here for all of it, but you're here now, and I believe we can make headway. Thank you for giving up your leave."

"You would do the same for me, I know." She pulled her coat more tightly around her. "But, my God, it's cold."

4

CRIME SCENE

Reid's Close was empty, save for the police cordon and a few chalk markings left on the road.

Tasha extracted an envelope from her bag containing two enlarged photographs. "Mack was lying on his back when they found him. His legs had twisted to his right side when he fell." She pointed to the ground near the middle of the close, holding up a photograph for the DI to compare.

Yvonne knelt next to the chalk markings.

Tasha continued. "Blood had soaked through most of his clothing and streamed down the alley there." She pointed along to the drain.

The DI shuddered. The tenements seemed to close in around her, adding to the weight and horror of what had occurred in the darkness only nights before. "Do they have CCTV?" She tilted her head, still comparing the scene in the photograph to their surroundings and imagining Mack's last moments. "It wasn't a robbery, given they left the wallet in the alley."

"They have CCTV of Mack and, separately, footage of

the person they believe was his attacker. However, they don't have the attack itself, unfortunately. Mack seemed to hang about for a while, and no-one is sure why."

Yvonne cast her gaze over the buildings. At one end of the alley, a covered exit led to Holyrood Road. The backs of the Victorian tenements walled the rest of the alley. "And this is part of the Royal Mile?"

"It is," Tasha affirmed. "We're close to the Scottish parliament." She pulled a face. "Hard to believe they murdered my friend so close to the Scottish seat of government."

"Murder is no respecter of position." Yvonne sighed. "How are you feeling, Tasha? This must be hard for you..."

"It's still sinking in." She hung her head. "It's going to take a while."

"Of course." The DI pushed her hands deep inside her coat pockets.

"So, what are your first impressions?" Tasha placed the photographs back in her bag.

Yvonne pursed her lips. "For me, the striking feature is the cocktail stick in the Eye. The killer placed it so precisely in the centre of the pupil. That has to be significant for the killer, but I can't help feeling it may be a message for someone else."

"I agree. The question is, does it have a more specific meaning?"

"It is one of the strangest murder signatures I have seen."

"But for whose benefit? His? The public? Police? Or someone else who attended the gathering that evening?"

"That's what we need to find out. The murder was likely premeditated. Do we know if Mack ever complained of being followed? Particularly, any time during the last few weeks of his life?"

Tasha scratched her head. "I don't know. We can ask

McKenzie that sort of thing. We won't be working in the dark. Grant said we can join his team and involve ourselves fully in the investigation."

"That was good of him."

"This is the bottom of the Royal Mile, next to Holyrood Park. The locals call it Queen's Park, apparently. Worth remembering if anyone mentions it under that name."

"Do you know if there have been any other murders in the area? Especially, with similarities to Mack's killing?"

"Mackenzie says not."

"I see..." the DI fell silent, her face pensive as they began the walk back through Canongate and Holyrood Road. To their left, towering concrete panels protected the back of Holyrood, the Scottish parliament, from attack. It reminded her of the threats faced by those in authority as the world became increasingly polarised, such as vehicles being used as either bombs or battering rams.

She linked her arm through Tasha's as they walked and pondered Trevor Macpherson's murder. Words were neither uttered nor necessary.

THE MAJOR INVESTIGATIONS TEAM, or MIT as it was more commonly known, worked out of Leith station. A slate-grey Victorian building, it overlooked the cobbled Charlotte Street. Yvonne mused the facade was not unlike that of the old police station in Aberystwyth, back in Wales.

Built in 1928, as the sheriff's court and town hall, they had converted it to a police station in 1968. It still boasted the grey-marble staircase and grand meeting room, formerly the debating chamber. The walls sported oil paintings in gilt frames and the occasional stained-glass window. An Alexander Cary painting entitled 'The landing of King George the IV, dominated the main wall.

A breathless McKenzie met them in reception. "Sorry I couldn't be with you earlier, we're flat out." He led them upstairs. "I must sort you with temporary access cards so you can come and go as you please."

"That would be helpful." Tasha said, walking behind him.

Yvonne felt like an interloper. She wasn't sure she could be useful this far out of her comfort zone.

A staircase and corridor later, they reached the main incident room, where the Scottish SIO introduced them to the other members of his team.

"This is DC Graham Dalgliesh, DC Helen McAllister, and DS Susan Robertson," McKenzie stepped back.

Yvonne and Tasha shook each of their hands.

DC Dalgliesh looked to be the oldest of the team members at around forty. The female detectives, Yvonne estimated to be mid-thirties.

McAllister said little, but Yvonne knew she was being appraised by an astute mind, behind the stylish thin-framed glasses.

McKenzie continued. "We have split our unit in two at the moment because of a separate murder enquiry we are involved in, the result of a domestic dispute. We found blood traces in the family home but, as yet, haven't found a body." He held his arms out. "So, for the moment, this is it. This everybody we have available for the Trevor Macpherson inquiry." He turned to Yvonne and Tasha. "So, if you two are serious about helping, we'd be keen to have you on board."

Yvonne winced. "I only have a couple of weeks, I'm

afraid. This is technically my leave. I'll be due back in the last week of November."

McKenzie nodded. "That's fine. You probably won't be around for the capture, but I'll appreciate any insights you may have while you're here."

"I can be here for the duration," Tasha made eye contact with Yvonne.

Her partner gave her a two-lidded wink, a show of understanding and support.

The psychologist smiled in acknowledgment.

On the board, the team had amassed the strands of evidence, the knowns and unknowns of the case so far.

Yvonne examined the closeup photographs of Mack's body, her gaze lingering on the cocktail stick in the eye of the dead man.

"It took time to do that," she announced.

"Sorry?" McKenzie glanced at the photo.

"The cocktail stick, I mean. He delivered the slashes and stabs at speed. They were frenzied. But, the cocktail stick? He was slow and meticulous with that. It would have taken time, and a steady hand."

McKenzie nodded. "I agree. It's a signature. A sign-off to the murder. We're expecting the full autopsy report later today. We'll have the pathologist's take on it. But, yes, I don't think this was a random killing. Our murderer did this to send a message. He got satisfaction from delivering that message."

"Was Mack ever involved in cases here in Edinburgh?" Yvonne asked.

McKenzie shook his head. "The first we ever saw of him was in that alley in Reid's Close. He didn't work with any of us."

"I see."

"We're interviewing his friends and analysing the forensic evidence we have. If he had enemies, those closest to him ought to know who they were. The killer also took the time to clean the weapon on his victim's clothing. He's one cool customer. He wasn't worried about anybody seeing him."

"That could be the Covid lockdown." Yvonne pursed her lips. "Most people are indoors, although he risked being seen by someone through the window."

"Uniform questioned the residents in those tenements. Not one of them saw anything."

"We have extra uniformed officers on the streets, now." Graham Dalgliesh rubbed his chin. "Should put him off trying something like this again."

"He seemed to know where the CCTV cameras were." Helen McAllister crossed over to the whiteboard, tucking her shoulder-length blonde hair behind her ears as she peered at the photos. It was a lighter blonde than Yvonne's. Ash, instead of straw.

"Did anyone leave the party with Mack?" Yvonne narrowed her eyes, hands in her skirt pockets.

"Not according to those who were there. Mack left on his own. Shortly after, Tom Frasier left." McKenzie cleared his throat. "However, they couldn't agree on the time. You know what it's like when alcohol is involved. And, they'd consumed a lot that afternoon and evening. We'll be carrying out formal interviews with all of those who were there in the coming days."

"Who found the body?" Yvonne leaned back against a desk.

"A routine patrol called it in. They stayed at the scene until SOCO and ourselves got there." He sighed. "We have one potential assailant on CCTV, but we don't have the face. The person was in dark clothing and kept their head turned away from the cameras, or bowed. The CCTV operator followed him for a short distance as the suspect passed through Holyrood Road, heading towards St Margaret's Loch area. But, they decided there was nothing going on, and something happening elsewhere caught their attention. We are having the footage enhanced and cleaned up, but I am not convinced we will get anything more from it."

"It's a start." Yvonne rubbed her lips, deep in thought.

"Would you like to be present when we conduct the interviews with the other partygoers?" McKenzie asked her.

She nodded. "I would, if that's okay?"

"Of course." He smiled. "It would be good to have your perspective. You can watch some of them from the viewing room. Will that be all right?"

"Not a problem." She grinned. "I am the interloper. I am more than happy to be an observer."

"Great." He checked his watch. "Time for a quick cuppa before we push on."

The DI had drunk nothing since her coffee at breakfast. Having rushed her sandwich with Tasha at the loch, her water bottle lay unopened in her bag. She needed that cuppa before she perused the initial statements of Mack's friends.

THAT EVENING, Tasha took Yvonne up to Arthur's Seat as the light was fading. "I'm sorry we didn't get to do this in daylight." Tasha threw her arms wide. "But, look..."

Below them lay the city, the orange glow of the street and window lights commingled with the brighter, sharper,

LEDS of cars and signs. A landscape made of light, and lines, and towering edifices.

It had taken them the best part of twenty-five minutes to climb the extinct volcano after leaving the car at Dunsapie Loch, the next loch up from St. Margaret's. This was the easier route to the summit, but the incline was steep, leaving them both panting.

"What a sight..." Yvonne stood, hands on hips, her breath making clouds in the evening air.

"We'll do it again in daylight, and take the longer route next time," the psychologist promised.

Yvonne allowed her gaze to wander from the silhouetted crags, formed from dolerite magma, to the evening city stretched into the distance below. "I can see Christmas lights."

"It's that time of year." Tasha put her chin on Yvonne's shoulder. "I wonder what Santa's going to bring you this year?"

"Santa?" Yvonne leaned her head against her partner's. "I have everything I need right here."

Tasha kissed her cheek. "I hope you always feel that way."

"I will."

The psychologist's expression darkened. "I wonder if Mack ever came here at dusk?"

"I should think he would have." Yvonne took Tasha's hand. "I bet he did many times. How could he not?"

"I never asked him, you know, about his home city. I knew he hailed from Edinburgh. His broad accent was a constant reminder, and I loved it. It's such a friendly dialect. I knew he intended moving back here after retirement, but I never got around to asking him about his home. Now, I can't understand why I didn't... Why I never took the time."

"Don't blame yourself, Tasha. We are all guilty of that. We assume we have years and years to explore the things we want to, and in the normal run of things, we do. But sometimes events take a different course, reminding us that time is a fragile, transient thing. What's solid now, can be vaporous tomorrow."

Tasha tilted her head. "That's deep."

"Death can leave one feeling... philosophical, don't you think?"

"Yes..."

It was fully dark by the time they returned to their hire car at Dunsapie Loch.

Tasha used a small magnum torch to light their way down, chiding herself for not buying something bigger. The going was slow, but safe enough in their walking boots.

When they got back to the room, they kicked off those boots and made mugs of hot chocolate to warm up.

Tasha ordered pasta for their evening meal. "I'm glad you came, Yvonne. It didn't feel right, being here without you."

The DI stood beside her as the psychologist poured them each a glass of house white. "Of course I came, why would I not? I missed you."

5

TWISTED CIPHER

"According to the pathologist, what we see here is very similar to the knife used." McKenzie pointed to the horrific weapon on the slide. "Known as the zombie knife, or head splitter."

The one shown had an ornate brass handle, was double-edged, and serrated. A line of holes patterned the middle of the blade.

"An illegal weapon, as you know. Ownership can get you four years in prison. It's not something we want on our streets. It's bad enough that it is out there at all. But now, a killer has used it on one of our own. The only purpose of this knife is violence and instilling fear. It has no other use The one shown has a seven-inch blade, similar to the one used to murder Trevor Macpherson. It creates nightmarish injuries, making it difficult or impossible for paramedics to save the lives of victims, even if they arrive on the scene in good time."

McKenzie put his hands deep in his trouser pockets, his expression grim. "We need to find this offender and his weapon, yesterday. I don't want either of them on the streets of Edinburgh any longer than necessary. In front of you is a copy of the pathology report." He referred to the document the team were passing between themselves. "The injuries to Macpherson were extensive and intended to be fatal. But then, the murderer did this..."

McKenzie's next slide was a closeup of the cocktail stick protruding from the left eye. "What was that about? What message was this meant to convey? Helen?"

"Sir?"

"I want you to delve into the symbolism. Find out if we have seen before this, in actual life or literature. Is there a significance? What does it mean?"

"Sir..." DC Dalgliesh nodded towards the door.

"What is it?" McKenzie glanced at the receptionist hovering in the doorway.

"Thought you would want to see this, sir." He handed the DI an envelope addressed to The Major Investigations Unit, Leith, Edinburgh. All in capital letters.

McKenzie donned two pairs of latex gloves before taking the contents from the already opened letter.

"I'm sorry." The receptionist grimaced. "I didn't know it might be evidence. I wouldn't have op-"

McKenzie held up his hand. "It's fine. We can eliminate your prints." He ran his hands through his hair. "I think this is from Mack's killer. He's claiming responsibility for the murder, stating that there are more details in this..." He held up a second piece of paper so they could see it. "It looks like a cipher. A coded message."

He laid the paper out flat, taking photographs of it and the envelope, before placing them in an evidence bag. "This needs to go to the labs, now." He handed the signed bag to the receptionist, along with a note to the forensic team.

"Yes, sir." The receptionist left the room.

McKenzie peered at his mobile. "Well, I'm no expert, but I'd say the symbols are a mix of Greek letters, random shapes, and hieroglyphs. I'll share it with you all via email. See what you make of it." He glanced at Yvonne and Tasha. "Do you have work phones with you?"

The DI nodded. "I do."

"Great. I will attach it to a message for you to look over at your convenience. I'm sure I don't need to tell you not to discuss the contents with anyone outside of this room, except for forensic services."

"Of course."

"Good. What's your number?"

She read it out to him.

"Know anything about ciphers?" He asked her after the briefing.

She shook her head. "I haven't dealt with one before, if that is what you mean?"

He pursed his lips. "Neither have we."

Tasha joined them. "Didn't the Zodiac use them to taunt the San Francisco police and newspapers, during his serial-killing spree in the nineteen-sixties?"

"He did." Yvonne nodded. "I don't think they deciphered all of them, even with the help of the army and intelligence services."

The psychologist nodded. "That's right. They didn't, but the ones they decrypted, were simple homophonic substitutions, if memory serves. Each symbol represented a letter. The Zodiac made it more complex, by using multiple symbols for the more common letters like E. I think he used up to five different symbols to represent the same letter. After they cracked the first one, he made his others more difficult. They were no longer simple homophonic substitutions. The killer mixed up his methods and, yes, some are still unsolved to this day."

"You'll need a code-breaker, Grant." Yvonne tilted her head. "Someone who can work out what sort of cipher you're dealing with. There are probably computer programmes to deal with codes, these days. That supposes this *is* from killer, and not a crank..."

"It's from the killer." McKenzie sighed. "He mentions the cocktail stick in the accompanying letter. That's a detail of the crime scene not divulged to the press or the public. It's him, all right. I'll pass this code to SCD, see what they say."

Yvonne knew he was referring to the Specialist Crime Division, the intelligence arm of Police Scotland.

He continued. "In the meantime, we can have a crack at it ourselves, in any spare moments. A few coffee breaks and sleepless nights and we might have an answer." He grinned, but it turned to a frown. "Joking aside, I don't like how this is shaping up."

Yvonne shook her head. "Neither do I."

∽

TREVOR MACPHERSON HAD several close friends, but relatively few acquaintances.

Yvonne clicked her tongue as she read the details of his life, gleaned from neighbours. "Aside from the friends he'd known since school, and those within the Met, he kept himself to himself. He hadn't contacted his ex-wife for several years. I think he would have felt very lonely living in that flat."

Tasha handed Yvonne a coffee. "His parents are dead. They passed away within six months of each other, several years ago."

The DI sipped the fiery liquid. "MacKenzie's team is liaising with the Met about the cases Mack worked. They're trawling through offenders who could be bearing a grudge." She turned to her partner. "You're not aware of anyone like that, are you?"

Tasha shook her head. "Mack was always fair. There weren't many who took exception to him, even amongst the more serious criminals he helped put behind bars. There was a respect for him amongst the underworld. However..." She shrugged. "That world is an ever-changing place. Who knows?"

Yvonne laid out a printed version of the killer's letter and cipher.

It read:

TO WHOM IT MAY CONCERN,

I AM THE KILLER OF THE POLICE OFFICER IN REID'S CLOSE.

I PUT THE WOOD IN HIS EYE.

HOPE YOU LIKED THAT TOUCH.

THE POET.

∽

"IT'S A POEM," Yvonne said aloud, as McKenzie joined them.

"A what?" Tasha frowned.

"He signed his letter The Poet, and he has organised his cipher into blocks that resemble the stanzas of a poem."

McKenzie perused the code. "You know, I think you could be right."

"It might help crack it." Yvonne leaned back. "Depending on his beats, we know that certain of the words will probably rhyme."

Tasha's face lit up. "Well spotted. That gives us a reasonable starting point."

McKenzie grinned at Yvonne. "Do you think your DCI would mind if we poached you?"

She laughed. "I am sure there are days when he would pay you to take me off his hands."

"I doubt that."

"Do you know of any criminals in the area who may be into poetry? Write poetry?"

He shook his head. "No-one comes to mind. I'll ask Dalgliesh. He's pretty good with that things like that."

"You could enquire with the Met, too?"

"I'll get McAllister onto that."

She nodded. "I have a feeling The Poet expects you to know who he is. He's going to taunt us until we figure it out."

McKenzie nodded. "SOCO got a partial print from Macpherson's cheek. Could belong to his killer."

"He touched him without gloves?" Yvonne frowned. "I didn't expect that."

"Me neither." McKenzie sighed. "Trouble is, they don't think they have enough points in the print to identify the perp. We can rule people out, but we can't convict on what we have."

"Just a thought..." Tasha scratched her chin.

"Go on," McKenzie prompted.

"I agree with Yvonne that the insertion of a cocktail stick so precisely into the centre of the eye would require far more care than stabbing than we might expect from a random murder. Perhaps, after Mack was lying defenceless, the killer removed a glove to carry out that last act. He was sloppy and left the partial because he was being so particular with the placement."

"I like your thinking." McKenzie nodded. "Jeezo, you two

can come again." He grinned at them. "I hope you're not planning on leaving soon."

Yvonne laughed. "As you know, I have to go back after next week, but I assume your scenes of crime will rule out prints from other partygoers. One of them may have touched his cheek before the killer attacked him."

"Aye, they'll be checking all that, and we're interviewing those who were at that gathering again, here in Leith. If someone so much as laid a finger on him at that party, we'll know about it."

Tasha pursed her lips. "I wouldn't mention the partial print anywhere. If he kills again, and he removes his gloves for the ultimate act, you may get a better print next time."

Yvonne nodded. "Someone at that party, either knowingly or unknowingly, must have given the killer information about Mack's whereabouts. The assassin knew where Mack would be, and when. Someone supplied those details. That had to be one of those at the gathering. There is nothing to suggest that Mack was in contact with anyone else."

Tasha nodded. "I agree. If this was a targeted murder, and I think we agree it doesn't appear to be a random one, then someone at that gathering has blood on their hands. The question is, who?"

6

STRANGE PLANS

Mack's flat was in the Edinburgh suburb of Portobello, three miles from the city centre.

Yvonne knew why the area would appeal to a man retiring from a life of chasing down the hardest and most frightening serial offenders in Britain.

After decades of horror-filled dreams, and disturbed sleep, Portobello, with its long promenade and spacious beaches of soft sand, could wash a mind clean with the soothing to-and-fro of the sea.

She closed her eyes. Yes, she knew why this place had been right for Trevor Macpherson.

"Are you ready?" Tasha asked, from somewhere behind.

The DI opened her eyes. "Yes." The world came back into focus.

A SOCO officer held up the yellow crime scene tape, allowing them to enter the Georgian building, accessed via a door to the right of the dentist's office, directly beneath Mack's flat.

A narrow, duck-egg-blue, carpeted staircase with bare

walls led to the two-bedroom apartment which the detective had purchased upon his retirement.

The stairs stopped at a narrow hallway, off of which branched two rooms to the left and three to the right.

There were black-and-white stills in plastic frames, photographs from Mack's childhood, arranged in rows along the left-hand wall of the corridor. The access was so narrow, they had to go single file.

Off to the left were Mack's lounge and kitchen, respectively. To the right, lay two bedrooms and a bathroom.

They entered the lounge first. The spacious room, lit via two sash windows, had been painted slate-grey. Against this backdrop, a tan leather suite caught the eye. An articulated floor lamp hung over one armchair.

The art on the walls, like the photographs in the hall, were also in black plastic frames.

An Ercol coffee table and Sideboard, and mustard-yellow rug, finished the sparse decor.

The flat was elegant and pleasing to the eye.

"He had good taste." Yvonne moved to one side, allowing the psychologist to enter.

Tasha nodded. "I'm not surprised. He was always neatly turned out, and the pens on his desk had to be just so. Mack was a meticulous man."

The DI crossed over to the first of the windows. It overlooked the communal garden at the back. Trees, grass, and shrubs, all neatly trimmed; the garden path, free from weeds. There were no flowers, and no borders for any. A bench sat under a pergola, next to a large acer. A clematis covered most of the wooden structure.

"Mack loved reading in his garden." Tasha sighed. "I can imagine him sitting on that bench."

Yvonne squeezed her partner's elbow. A gentle show of support. "Come on, the kitchen is next door."

Tasha wiped a finger across her eyes and followed the DI to the next room.

Unlike the rest of the flat, the kitchen could have done with an overhaul. The white cupboards were practical but plain, several doors hanging awry. It was tidy, however. No dishes in the sink. Nothing on the drainer.

"He didn't even leave a dirty mug before he went out." Yvonne pursed her lips.

"The bedroom is in a mess." Tasha called from the corridor.

The DI joined her, opening her mouth in surprise at the unmade bed and discarded underwear on the floor. Two shirts lay in a heap on top of the bed. Perhaps he had tried them on, for the birthday gathering, on the night he died. They hadn't made the cut.

The bedroom window overlooked the street. In the distance, over the rooftops, they could glimpse the sea.

A desk in one corner of the room contained maps of Edinburgh and a set of plans, the subject of which was not immediately obvious.

"He let it all hang out in here." Tasha joined Yvonne at the desk.

The DI nodded. "His safe space. Did he have an interest in maps?"

The psychologist shook her head. "Not that I am aware."

Yvonne ran a gloved hand over the map of Edinburgh. "I wonder what he was thinking?"

"McKenzie said they found a notebook. It's with SOCO. There weren't any obvious clues in it, but someone had torn out pages. They're examining them for telltale indentations."

"Perhaps he knew he was in danger. Maybe he lost his life because of something he knew. Something he found out."

Tasha nodded. "When Mack got his teeth into a case, he'd keep digging, no matter the peril."

"Bathroom?"

They passed the second bedroom, full to the rafters with furniture and discarded items. Clearly, Mack had used it for storage after downsizing from his much bigger London apartment.

The bathroom was the smallest room in the place. Modern in styling and clean.

The DI flicked open the cabinet, finding only a toothbrush and toothpaste, shaving items and paracetamol. "Did you tell me Mack separated from his wife?" she asked Tasha.

"They divorced, Yvonne. About fifteen years ago. His wife ran off with someone she met at work. She's a physics teacher in London. He remained friends with her, though they barely saw one another. They had tried for years, before the split, to have children. It didn't work out. Mack felt he was to blame because of all the overtime he spent working cases. It took him a long time to get over the breakup."

The DI sighed. "Poor guy."

"He didn't meet anyone else. He seemed to lose interest in having a relationship and plunged himself ever more into his work. You would be hard-pressed to find anyone more dedicated."

"Once a detective, always a detective." The DI wandered back to Mack's bedroom, and the maps.

"Sorry?" Tasha followed her, raising her brows.

"I think he might have been working another case. Moonlighting, on something that got him killed."

The psychologist tilted her head. "That sounds like Mack, and he wouldn't have been one to let go once he had the bit between his teeth, either. Question is, what might that case have been?"

"There you are!" A broad Scottish voice boomed from the doorway. Grant McKenzie filled the frame. "What are you two thinking?"

"I'm curious about the maps and plans, Grant." Yvonne leaned over the desk, her eyes scanning the paperwork.

He joined her. "What about them?"

"Well, there are two maps of Edinburgh, a city he already knew very well, and these..." She ran a gloved hand over one of the unlabelled plans.

McKenzie peered at them. "I wonder..."

"What?" She narrowed her eyes.

"Well, if I'm not mistaken, this is Faslane." He lifted the map to peer more closely at it. "It's the right layout, and this here is the water."

"Faslane? Isn't that a military base?"

"A naval base, yes. It's one of the most secure on the planet. They have nuclear submarines based there. It's on the Gare Loch."

"Why would Mack have plans of Faslane?"

He shrugged. "Beats me." He glanced at Tasha. "Was he a military buff? It looks like he printed these from the internet."

Tasha shook her head. "Not that I know of." She frowned. "And I'm fairly sure he would have said something to me about it, if he was. He told me all sorts. I'm positive he'd have mentioned it."

McKenzie checked his watch. "They have photographed everything, but SOCO officers are still coming in and out, as and when they need to. I'll get them to bag these up for us."

Yvonne took a few snaps with her mobile. "I don't think he had these because he was into the military. I think he was working on something. If you look at his bookcase over there, I don't see a single book on the army or navy."

He nodded. "I agree. We should find out why he had those plans."

She placed her mobile in her bag. "Another question to ask his closest friends."

7

SUSPECT PARTY

Five others had been at the gathering in The Royal Mile the night Trevor Macpherson lost his life. All had broken the strict Covid rules set out by the Scottish parliament, designed to limit the spread of the pandemic's second wave. Those rules decreed that there were to be no meetings between people from more than the two households that were in so-called bubbles, and that any gathering indoors between those households was further limited to six persons.

McKenzie had asked each of the five friends to attend Leith police station, intimating that cooperation with the investigation into Mack's death would lead to a waiving of the fines they faced for breaking the lockdown rules. Non-cooperation, however, would mean facing the full penalty.

The first of the interviews was with fifty-eight-year-old bookseller, Michael Muirhouse. His bijou, well-patronised store stood in Broad Street, in Edinburgh's Royal Mile, a short walk from where a killer had brutally slain the ex-detective.

Muirhouse Books had a reputation for performing miracles, when sourcing first and special editions, for those with enough money to pay for them. Michael had done very well for himself since growing up in the working class area with which he shared his surname.

He attended the station in a shirt and tie over which he wore a long sheepskin coat.

Five-feet-nine, broad-shouldered, and straight-backed, he exuded easy confidence, and was not afraid of making eye-contact with DI McKenzie and DS Robertson.

DS Susan Robertson wore her long, auburn hair in a tight bun. Her slender frame and lean features lent her a stern, no messing, air.

Yvonne and Tasha observed through a two-way mirror which took up almost half of one wall.

Although the interview was being recorded with Muirhouse's blessing, the DI made notes as the interview progressed.

McKenzie kicked things off. "Can you tell us how you came to be at the gathering in Canongate? What were you told about the event?"

Muirhouse screwed his eyes up, as though struggling to remember. "Och, let's see... It was Jack Hendry's sixtieth birthday bash. We planned it months before the first lockdown for the coronavirus. We had wanted to do a pub crawl and go for a meal. We changed the plans when we found ourselves in the middle of a pandemic, with a bunch of new rules."

"Okay." McKenzie cleared his throat. "Why did you ignore the ban on gatherings?"

Muirhouse sighed. "To be honest, everyone was suffering from lockdown fatigue. There was disagreement even between the different governments in the UK, as to what they wanted people to do regarding the second wave and, honestly, I was sick of it. So were many others. We agreed that once we had celebrated Jack's birthday we would behave ourselves and wait until lockdown ended before we got together again. Mack, God rest his soul, organised the party, but he was one of those most uncomfortable with breaking lockdown rules. We persuaded him, however." Muirhouse sighed. "Of course, in hindsight, I wish we hadn't. But we couldn't have foreseen what would happen to him."

"So, it was Mack who suggested the get-together?" DS Robertson held Muirhouse's gaze.

"Initially, yes, but it was em..." He screwed his eyes up again, angling his face towards the ceiling, before bringing them back to the detectives. "Kenny Balfour's idea to go ahead with it during lockdown. We knew that Douggie Cameron would rent a hotel room. And we thought it would be a good idea to hold it there because we could use the bar. But, with further restrictions in place, we decided we could only have six of us together if we used the fire escape, kept the party quiet, and raided the minibar. We also took a few bevvies with us."

"Where were the hotel staff?" McKenzie asked.

"We didn't see any. The fire escape was right next to Douggie's room. As far as I knew, the hotel was running a skeleton staff, with many on furlough because of vastly reduced numbers of tourists. To be honest, I'm surprised no-one came to see us. There was a CCTV camera out the back. I thought they would have clocked us, but maybe they weren't checking it because there was hardly anyone about. Anyway, no-one came to speak to us."

"What about music? Wouldn't they have heard that?"

Muirhouse shook his head. "We didn't have loud music. We had some oldies playing on Jack's phone. That was about it. There was no chance the hotel reception staff would have heard it, and we put a blanket over the doorframe to help dampen the sound. If they heard us, they obviously didn't feel like doing anything about it." He laughed. "Probably grateful for the money they'd get from the minibar."

McKenzie tutted. "And people wonder why this second wave is kicking off so fast..."

Up in the interview room, Yvonne pressed her lips tightly together, not impressed with Muirhouse's attitude. She turned to Tasha. "His body language is open, but something's not right about him."

"I agree." Tasha nodded. "What I'm curious about, is his pretence at struggling to remember crucial details. Someone murdered one of his best friends that night. There's no way he wouldn't remember whose idea the party was. His acting is a little over the top for my liking."

Yvonne folded her arms, head tilted in thought. "I agree. I think he knows more than he's letting on. I wonder if someone tipped members of staff so they wouldn't report them? I think it unlikely they didn't know what was going on in that room."

"Muirhouse has a point, though." Tasha sighed. "These are hard times. They may have been willing to turn a blind eye for the extra revenue from the minibar."

McKenzie levelled a steely gaze at Muirhouse. "How did Mack seem to you during the party? And how was he when he left?"

"Again, he said he needed to get back as he didn't want to be out too late because of restrictions, but he seemed fine in himself. He didn't look upset or worried about anything."

"No agitation?"

Muirhouse shook his head. "I didn't see any. I wasn't

watching him that closely, though. I mean, we were all just chatting and laughing."

"So, the others were in good spirits? Did anyone appear quiet? Broody?"

"No, not that I could see, Inspector."

McKenzie put his pen down. "Did you, or anyone you know, have anything to do with Trevor Macpherson's death?"

"No."

"Are you sure about that?"

For the first time, Muirhouse scowled. "Of course I am. We were friends."

McKenzie pushed back his chair. "You're free to go, Mister Muirhouse. Don't leave Edinburgh. We may want to speak with you again."

∽

THEY INTERVIEWED KENNY BALFOUR NEXT, another of the five friends, and the alleged organiser of the illegal gathering in the hotel.

He had dressed up for the occasion, but looked uncomfortable in his dog-eared yellow tie, and long-collared denim shirt which could have been purchased in the eighties. He frequently smoothed his slicked-back, grey-peppered hair, tucking it behind his ears, wiping the sweat from his upper lip with hands which he dried on his corduroys.

"Mr Balfour," McKenzie began. "Thank you for coming in at such brief notice."

"Aye, that's no problem." Kenny let out a shuddering sigh, the kind designed to slow a speeding heart.

"Ken... Can I call you that?"

"Aye, it's Kenny."

"Kenny, I understand you arranged the get-together for Jack Hendry's sixtieth birthday?"

Kenny's shoulders rose as though he wanted his head to disappear down the neck of his shirt. "I suggested we do it at the hotel, yes." He grimaced. "There weren't any restrictions when I organised it, you know?"

"Aye, we know." McKenzie held up his land. "Look, we can talk about Covid another time. To be frank, if you tell us everything you know, we'll ignore the Covid violations that occurred that night. We want Trevor Macpherson's murderer. We need your help to get him."

DS Robertson joined in. "This was a heinous crime, Kenny. We need Mack's killer and his murder weapon off the streets."

Kenny fiddled with his hair, sweat beading on his forehead. "Tell me what you want to know. I didn't see the murder." Enlarged pupils made his eyes appear black.

"How did Mack seem to you, that night?" McKenzie glanced through his notes. "Was he his usual self? Was there anything different about him? Did anything strike you as odd about his behaviour?"

Kenny thought about it, his eyes losing focus as he pictured the party in his mind. "Not really, except..."

"Except what?" The Scottish DI leaned in. "What are you thinking?"

"Well, he drank more than I thought he would. Or, I should say, he drank faster than I'd seen him drink before. He really knocked them back, and that wasn't like Mack. He was generally a slower drinker than the rest of us. He would take his time, you know?"

"But he didn't that night?"

"No. He had three drinks to my one, I would say. Usually,

it would be the other way around. I normally drank way more than Mack."

"Did he tell you something was bothering him? Mention any troubles to you? Was he concerned for himself or others?"

Kenny shook his head. "No, but even if he had been stressed, he wouldn't have thought it appropriate to mention it at a mate's birthday night. Mack wasn't the kind to put a downer on something. He was a solid guy. One of the best."

"You'd known him since school, I understand?"

"Aye, we grew up together. We were from the same street in Muirhouse Our fathers worked in the same factory. We were always close. Of course, we lost touch while he was working in London, but we always knew in the back of our minds that the friendship was there. That we'd catch up again. We were sound."

"Did Mack talk to you about how he found it, settling back in Edinburgh again, after London? Was it easy? Difficult?"

"As far as I know, he found it easy, right enough. I mean, I think he missed his work in London. He was sometimes at a loss about what to do with his time, but he told me he was enjoying retirement, and that he'd been ready for it. He had tired of the cut and thrust, but I think anyone would take a while to adjust after a long career in a different city. I struggled after retiring early because of my bad back, and I didn't have to move cities. I couldn't do the heavy lifting my job required any more. I was glad of the rest, but I missed my workmates."

"What about the others at the party? How did they seem? Were they settled? Happy? Did you witness any tension? Atmospheres?"

Kenny shook his head. "Nothing obvious, that I saw.

The Edinburgh Murders

Everyone was having a good time. We had a bit of a sing-song, put a cover over the door to stop some noise from getting to the corridor. But, I think they would have heard us, anyway. Especially, as the evening went on. I think we got louder and louder. You ken what it's like when guys get drunk together."

"Sure." McKenzie nodded. "And, you didn't see anyone else? Anyone from outside of the party? Staff? Any other hotel guests?"

"No." Kenny was firm. "No-one. It surprised me. I felt sure the hotel staff would come after us about the racket we were making, or because there were so many people in the room, but they left us alone."

"I understand Mack was the first to leave the party-"

"He wasn't." Kenny snapped his eyes to McKenzie's. "He wasn't the first to leave."

The detective frowned. "But, I thought-"

"Tom left first."

"Tom Frasier?"

"Aye."

"Are you sure about that?"

"Och, aye, I'm sure."

"How long before Mack, did Frasier leave?"

"Och, God, now you're asking... I would say around twenty minutes, or so."

"Can you be sure of that?"

"Well, I checked my watch when Tom left. I had been sure it was earlier than it was. I was going to tell him he was a lightweight, thinking it was around six-thirty, but it was nine o'clock. It surprised me it had got so late. We started early because we knew there was a curfew from ten o'clock. I thought Tom was being a party-pooper."

"And Mack left twenty minutes later?"

"Aye, about that."

"So, about nine-twenty?"

"Aye."

"Could you be wrong about the time? Given that, as you say yourself, the time was racing by?"

"I'm pretty sure it was only about twenty minutes. Once Tom left, I was more aware of the time, because I was disappointed that it was disappearing so fast."

"How much had you had to drink by then?"

"Och, let's see, I'd had about four cans of strong lager, and several drams of whiskey."

"Would you describe yourself as drunk?"

"No, I'd say I was tipsy, but I not drunk. I can take my liquor, Inspector. It'd take a few more pints than that to get me bladdered. I've drunk a few people under the table in my time, I can tell you."

"I see."

"That's how I can be fairly sure about the times. I was still with it, at nine o'clock."

"Do you know anything about codes, Kenny?"

"Codes?" Kenny's eyes narrowed. "What do you mean? Like keypad codes?"

"I mean writing in code? Cracking codes?"

Kenny pulled a face. "I can't say as I do. I mean, I've never used one, if that's what you're asking? I don't know anyone who has. Unless, you mean Morse Code?"

McKenzie chuckled. "I'm referring to ciphers."

"Ciphers?" Kenny screwed his face up.

"Never mind. Do you like poetry? Does anybody you know like poetry?"

"My mother liked poetry."

"Besides your mother?"

"No." Kenny wobbled his head.

"All right, Kenny. Thank you for coming in. We may need to speak with you again at some point."

"Aye, well, you know where I am."

"Thank you. DS Robertson will see you out."

~

IN THE OBSERVATION ROOM, Yvonne leaned back in her chair. "So, one of the guests left before Mack."

"Tom Frasier." Tasha pressed her lips together.

"Yes. Even if he wasn't the killer, he may have seen something. I wonder why he didn't tell us he left before Mack? What's he hiding?"

"He could be our killer or, perhaps, he's afraid he could be next on the killer's list? I can't wait to see what Frasier has to say."

Yvonne rubbed her chin. "I'm willing to bet that somebody at that gathering knows more than they have so far admitted. The question is, which one?"

~

DOUGLAS CAMERON, a fifty-seven-year-old publican from Glasgow, arrived for an interview in the afternoon, dressed in a suit jacket and an open shirt. His greying hair was fashionably short. He settled in his seat, like a man at ease. It did not surprise her he had been in the navy. She suspected he could take care of himself, even now.

Once again, McKenzie and Robertson were the interviewers. Yvonne and Tasha took up their places in the viewing room.

The Scottish DI pointed at the camera in the room's

corner, informing Cameron that they recorded all interviews.

The interviewee shifted in his seat. "That's fine," he said, eyeing the equipment for several seconds, crossing and uncrossing his legs.

"Thanks for coming in, Douggie. Can I call you that?"

"Yes, that's what my friends call me."

"I understand you were one of six people at Jack Hendry's birthday party, the night of the murder?"

"Yes, I was." Douggie tilted his head. "You've not found his killer, then?"

"Not yet. We were hoping you might help us."

Cameron shrugged. "Well, I can try. Depends what you need?"

"I understand you run a pub in Glasgow?"

"Yes, I do. The White Hart."

"How long have you been there?"

"Must be around five years, I think."

"How long had you known Mack?"

"Och, I've known... I knew Mack since we were teenagers. We became friends as youngsters. We'd have rammies with the boys from the neighbouring block. Those were the good old days."

"You're an ex-navy man?"

Cameron raised his brows. "I am. I was in the navy for twenty years."

"When did you leave?"

"Just over five years ago."

"Why did you leave?"

"The navy?"

"Yes."

"I resigned. I wanted to spend more time with my family. I have a wife and two sons. Both of my boys have left home, but they were still at university when I quit the navy. I wanted to be home for the holidays."

"Where were you based?"

Douggie studied McKenzie's face before answering. "Mostly, especially in later years, they based me at Faslane. I'm sorry, I don't see what that has to do with Mack's death? I don't think the navy had anything to do with it. Why do I feel you already know the answers to these questions?"

McKenzie folded his arms. "What was your job in the navy?"

Cameron frowned. "I was a cryptanalyst."

"Does that mean you worked with codes?"

"Deciphering them, yes."

"Interesting..."

"Why?"

"Do you write poetry?"

"What?"

"How did Mack seem to you, the night of the party?"

Cameron's expression softened. "He was in good spirits and having a great time. He was hellbent on making sure everyone else had a good time, too."

∽

IN THE OBSERVATION ROOM, Yvonne turned to Tasha. "So there is a link between Cameron and Faslane?"

Tasha nodded. "And he knows a lot about encryption."

"I hope Grant pushes him on that."

∽

McKenzie continued. "Did you notice anything, about Mack, that caused you concern? Was there any point at which he looked worried, or out of sorts?"

Cameron shook his head.

"What about drink? Did he consume more or less than he would at any other time?"

"I would say he drank about the same as he normally would. No more, no less."

"How was he when he left the gathering?"

"He was a little merry from the beer, but otherwise fine. He left early because of the Covid curfew. He didn't want to cause bother for the local police, having been an officer himself, you know?"

McKenzie nodded. "Makes sense. Do you know of anyone who might have wanted Mack dead?"

Cameron frowned. "No." His unblinking eyes pierced the detective.

"Did Mack ever ask you about your time at Faslane?"

"At the base?" Cameron shifted in his seat. "Not recently, no."

"So, he asked you a while back?"

"Maybe, when we were reminiscing, when I first came out of the navy. That was a few years ago. Why do you ask me that? Why would Mack be interested in Faslane?"

"Did he show an interest in navy matters?"

"Not that I know of, no. If he did, he didn't talk to me about it."

"Did he like poetry?"

"What is this interest in poetry?" Cameron scowled.

"Do you own any weapons? Like a zombie knife, otherwise known as a head splitter?"

"A head-splitter? Was that what they used on Mack? My God..."

"Yes."

"I didn't know that." Cameron's face softened. "Who makes those weapons? Poor Mack. Those knives seem to be everywhere these days. And, no, I don't own one. I have never owned such a weapon, and I didn't kill Mack. He was a friend. Whatever he was up to, he didn't discuss it with me. I'm sure he investigated, and put away, many nasty people over his career. Perhaps, start there."

"We know you didn't kill Mack. Your friends confirmed you were still at the party. If they are telling us the truth, your alibi is solid."

"Well, that's a relief." Cameron sighed.

"Did you see Mack leave?"

"I did, and I said goodbye to him. I believe I hugged him, too."

"You believe?"

"I did. I hugged him."

"Did anyone leave before him?"

Dougie frowned. "No."

"Not Tom Frasier?"

"Tom? No, I noticed Frasier wasn't there about half an hour after Mack left. That wasn't long before the rest of us made a move for home. But, I was deep in conversation with Jack Hendry and I was drunk, so I was a little oblivious. It is possible Tom left before Mack, but I didn't see him go. Mack attempted to say goodbye to me. That's how I know the time when he left. I was leery by then. You'd think, running my own bar, I could take my drink."

"And, being ex-navy," McKenzie tossed back.

"Aye but, as a publican, I've got used to not drinking so much. I'm far too busy supplying alcohol to others."

McKenzie nodded. "Of course. Is there anything else you would like to tell us, Douggie?"

Cameron shook his head. "Only that I'm sorry mack died. He was a good man with a big heart. We're really going to miss him."

"I'm sorry for your loss." McKenzie leaned back in his chair. "That will be all for now, but don't leave the country. We will probably speak with you again."

"You know where I am." Cameron stood, offering his hand for the detectives to shake.

Neither did.

McKenzie opened the door. "Sorry for your loss. We'll be in touch."

8

MURDER OF JUDGE ABERNATHIE

Judge John Abernathie removed his charcoal-grey pullover, feeling relief as the cool air reached his damp armpits.

Fingers drumming on the surface of the oak desk in his study, he flicked his eyes to the clock on the mantlepiece while the files downloaded from his laptop. It was eight o'clock.

He closed his hand over the memory stick, impatient for the transfer to finish. When it did, he pulled the stick out, snapping it into the lid that hung on a lanyard around his neck.

Time was running out. Abernathie selected the original folder on his laptop and hit delete, running a forefinger across his sweaty lip while letting out a shuddering sigh.

Grabbing his jacket from the back of the Chesterfield, he headed for the door. There wasn't a moment to lose.

Within forty minutes, he would be across the city and handing the files over. He could breathe easy once he had. It wouldn't be his problem anymore.

He backed his Range Rover out of the garage, closing the door with the remote on his dash.

Something was wrong. The steering was stiff. A squelching noise came from the left-hand side. He brought the car to a halt before it hit the street, jumping out to inspect the passenger side.

As he suspected, the tyre was flat. Protruding a few millimetres out of it was the head of a metal screw.

"Damnit!" He must have run over it the previous day. There was no option but to change the wheel.

Retrieving the jack from the garage, he manoeuvred it under the vehicle and started pumping.

He saw the blade long before he saw the man, letting go of the jack, he made a run for the garage.

The first slash caught him across the back. The second severed the bicep on his right arm just as he reached the garage and was trying to pull the shutter closed.

The following stab penetrated the judge's abdomen.

The figure in the skeleton mask pulled the knife back to thrust it in again.

John Abernathie couldn't feel pain anymore. The darkness came over him like a shroud. He sank into its sinister comfort, closing his eyes and crashing to the floor.

Somewhere above, a shout went up from a neighbouring property.

He tried opening his eyes, but oxygen-starved muscles refused.

Minutes later, the yard was awash with frantic activity, but Judge Abernathie had already gone.

∽

"Can you join us at Morningside?"

"Morningside? Where's that?"

"Get a pen and pad, I'll give you the postcode."

"What's happened?" Yvonne set down her untouched glass of chardonnay, glad she hadn't imbibed.

Grant McKenzie sighed on the other end. "We've got another murder, Yvonne. Same MO and signature. I would really value your input. Is Tasha with you? She's not answering her phone."

Yvonne looked across at her partner. "Yes, she's here with me."

"Great. Can you get yourselves here, ASAP?" He reeled off an address and postcode and the DI scribbled it down.

"It's a posh area, so come smart."

"What?"

McKenzie laughed. "Joke."

"Oh." She wasn't laughing. "We'll see you there, Grant."

Morningside was two-and-a-half miles from Edinburgh city centre.

Originally a farming village, it was now home to some of Edinburgh's wealthiest inhabitants, and populated by Edwardian and Victorian villas, tenements, detached and semi-detached houses.

The address they attended was a semi-detached residence south of the railway line. A villa split into two well-appointed homes.

The women parked their hire-car in an adjoining street, before walking past the cordons, police vehicles, and ambulances.

The place thronged with emergency personnel and armed officers. A helicopter droned overhead, its dazzling beam scouring the streets and gardens.

Tasha shuddered. "I hope they get him," she said, referring to the killer.

Yvonne nodded. "That would be great, but he won't have stuck around. He'll have had his escape route planned out. It'll be a miracle if they locate him tonight."

McKenzie was waiting for them, wearing his protective suit.

They grabbed their own plastic suits from the back of the SOCO van, putting them on as the Scottish detective prepared them for what they were about to see.

"The victim was a district judge, name of John Abernathie. The killer slashed and stabbed him several times in the driveway. There's no evidence the killer accessed the home. It looks like he attacked him here, then fled. No sign of the weapon either, but there are footprints in the victim's blood which look to be from a size eight training shoe. Neighbours thought they heard banging outside but, by the time they got here, the attacker had gone and the victim was no longer breathing. Two of the neighbours accessed the scene, and we have requested their shoes for elimination."

McKenzie led them down the gravelled driveway to a scene peppered by numbered markers as SOCO worked the scene. "We think he was in the middle of changing a flat tyre which a screw had pierced."

Yvonne looked over at the Range Rover, noting the blood spatter to the back of it.

Grant McKenzie continued. "There's a tyre iron lying next to the dead man. We think he tried to defend himself with it. It may have the perp's DNA."

Yvonne knelt near to the victim who lay on his back, his features relaxed. Only one of his eyes was open. It had a cocktail stick protruding from its pupil. "I've seen many victims with their ultimate horror etched on their face. Aside from the stick in his eye, this guy looks like he went to sleep."

McKenzie nodded. "Something tells me he was expecting trouble."

Yvonne's eye came to rest on the lanyard around the victim's neck, the lid of a memory stick dangling from it. "Looks like the killer got what he came for."

"Data..." McKenzie nodded. "We're taking Abernathie's laptop and mobile phone. Whatever was on that stick may still be on one of his machines."

Yvonne pursed her lips. Or maybe not. If it was so important they could kill him for it, he probably deleted whatever it was.

"Quite possible, but the labs may rescue something."

"I wonder where he was going?"

"Sorry?" McKenzie came closer as the drone of the helicopter and an approaching siren drowned her out.

"The Range Rover... The keys are in it. I wonder where the judge was going before he discovered this flat tyre?"

"Perhaps, to give someone that memory stick?"

Yvonne nodded. "Mack's murder may have spooked the Judge. They may have known each other."

"I think you are right." Tasha came to Yvonne's side. "The cocktail stick is the warning to others. Someone wanted these men silenced."

The DI pulled down her face mask. "We should find out who that memory stick was for before the killer does."

McKenzie's placed his hands on his hips. "We'll turn this place upside down and check out every contact we find."

9

A MAJOR SCOOP

Back in their hotel room, Yvonne scribbled notes, drawing a flowchart and timeline of events.

She poured over the things they were certain about, and the many questions still hovering over them. Like why Mack would keep aerial plans and photographs of Faslane naval base.

That he was working on something, she was fairly certain. The trouble was, they did not know what he had got himself into, and whether his friends had been aware of his circumstances. Did Mack and John Abernathie know each other? She suspected both men died because of something they knew. She also believed that someone at Jack Hendry's party knew more than they were letting on, and had given the killer, or killers, information on Mack's whereabouts.

"Penny for them?" Tasha, clad in thick flannel pyjamas, began massaging her shoulders.

"I have to go back in four days, Tasha. This feels like the worst time to leave, but I'm running out of time."

"Can't you ask Llewelyn for more leave? He'd understand, wouldn't he? It's not as though you make a habit of taking time out. I bet you're owed a lot more holiday than you have ever taken."

Yvonne shrugged. "I don't know. Current cases are stretching my team as it is. He wasn't entirely happy with me taking leave at short notice. He'll be even less happy about me asking to extend it."

"I know you." Tasha smiled, tilting her head. "Once you get the bit between your teeth on a case like this, you're not one to let go."

"You're right, I really don't want to leave this investigation now. Not when we're beginning to get somewhere." She turned to her partner. "You don't think this is a psychopath, do you? Do you agree with me that the victims were likely killed because of something they knew?"

"Definitely." Tasha frowned. "We should push McKenzie about the solution to the cipher. There will be clues in it about the motivation of the killer. It may tell us if he is a narcissistic madman, or someone who knows exactly what he is doing, and using murder to silence detractors."

∽

McKenzie's team prepped for Tom Frasier's interview, armed with the information gleaned from Kenny Balfour, that Frasier had left the gathering twenty minutes before Mack on the night he was murdered, something Frasier had not admitted when originally questioned.

The Scottish DI paced in front of the whiteboard. "At the very least, the Frasier may have seen something related to the murder, but it's quite possible he was responsible for it." He handed round a sheet with Frasier's known details. "And also, we know he is a writer and could be our poet."

Yvonne raised her eyebrows. "Does he write poetry?"

"Well, technically he's a journalist, but he's still a writer."

"Can I be in on the interview?"

McKenzie's eyes lit up. "I was hoping you would ask. If you hadn't, I might have had to beg." He grinned. "Och, in all seriousness, I'd value your input. Of all the people at that gathering, I think Tom Frasier has the most questions to answer." He turned to Tasha. "Can you watch his reactions from the viewing room? You may spot something we don't. I'll have an earpiece in so you can make suggestions."

"Of course."

"Great." He checked his watch. "He should be here any minute."

∽

AT SIX-FOOT-ONE, Tom Frasier towered above Yvonne. Clearly defined muscles stretched the fabric of his white shirt and dark trousers, the way his facial muscles stretched his skin. His narrowed eyes communicated intelligence.

Yvonne noted the crossed arms and legs, suspecting he might not give information readily. At least, not anything he didn't want to.

The Scottish DI kicked off the interview. "Thank you for coming in, Tom. Can I call you Tom?"

"Sure." Frasier nodded. "Most people do."

"How well did you know Trevor Macpherson?"

Frasier unfolded his arms. "Very. I'd known him since I was a boy. He was my godfather."

"Your godfather? I didn't know that."

"He was good friends with my father, Peter Frasier. My dad was killed in an oil rig accident in nineteen-ninety-seven. I was eight years old. Mack used to visit my mum and I. He'd buy me gifts at Christmas, and see us all right if we were running short of money. He couldn't replace my dad, no-one could do that. But I loved him like an uncle."

"Who invited you to the birthday gathering? Did you know Kenny Balfour?"

"I knew all the friends, vaguely, but it was Mack who invited me to the birthday do. In fact, the whole thing was really Mack's idea, although he left the final organising to Kenny. Mack had other things on his mind."

"What other things?" McKenzie leaned in.

Frasier shrugged. "I wouldn't know. He didn't tell me." He folded his arms again, eyes flicking to the clock.

"What do you do for a living, Tom?"

"Didn't I already tell officers what I did, the first time they questioned me? The officers in uniform?"

"We understand that you're a writer, but that can mean many things," Yvonne said, her eyes fixed on him. "We were hoping you'd be a little more specific."

Frasier frowned. "I'm a journalist. Freelance. I write articles for several papers and magazines, some of them, big nationals."

She nodded. "I thought I'd seen your name somewhere before." She hadn't, but hoped massaging his ego would help loosen his tongue.

He unfolded his arms. "I try to cover the important stuff. Things I think the public should know. The bigger issues."

"What are you working on at the moment?"

He stared at her, eyes narrowed.

She could tell he was weighing her up. Trying to work out where she was going with her questions.

"I'm working on a piece about the coronavirus, questioning the need for lockdown. I've been delving into the figures of cases and deaths in the UK and beyond."

"Are you working on anything else?"

He shook his head. His eyes flicked to the clock.

"Anything to do with Faslane?"

They snapped back to her face, to his hands, and slowly back to her. "Why would I be interested in Faslane?"

"I was hoping you would tell me. If you're not working on an article about the base, then you need only tell me that."

"But, that's a very specific question."

"I think Mack had developed an interest in Faslane, before he died."

Frasier shifted in his seat. A sheen developed on his upper lip. His cheeks paled.

She continued. "Did you know that? Did he discuss his interest with you?"

"A man can have an interest in anything he likes, can't he?"

She nodded, holding his gaze. "Of course. We only get involved if whatever he is into results in his death."

"You don't think..." He frowned.

"What?"

He laughed, but there were no creases around his eyes. "A chap doesn't get killed for taking an interest in the navy. You've got a vivid imagination, I'll give you that. You could be a writer, yourself."

She smiled. "But I'm not. I'm a police officer. I'll phrase the question differently. Do you know why Trevor Macpherson was taking an interest in the Faslane naval base?"

He shook his head.

"Is that a no?"

"Yes." His eyes flicked to the clock.

"What time did you leave the gathering at the hotel that night?"

He shrugged. "I didn't take notice of the time. I think... some time after nine?"

"Are you sure?"

"Well no, like I said, I didn't check the time."

She pursed her lips. "You're a journalist, and one who will be more than aware of the restrictions because of Covid, given the article you are working on. Am I right? I'd have thought you'd have checked your watch for that reason, if for nothing else?"

"I'm not a clock watcher." He scowled.

"Mr Frasier..." She licked her lower lip. "You have looked at our clock five times since we began this interview."

He leaned back, placing his hands on the top of his head.

"Your friends said you left before Mack. Is that right? Could you have left before him?" She could tell he was choosing his next words with care.

"It might be correct, aye, but even if it is, I didn't see Mack after I left the party. So, if that is what you're thinking, you're mistaken. I didn't see him, and I didn't kill him."

"Where did you go?" she asked, tapping her pen against her chin.

"I've changed my mind. I don't like where this is going. I'd like to speak with my solicitor."

"Very well." She glanced at McKenzie, who nodded. "Interview suspended, pending arrival of your solicitor."

10

A PLETHORA OF QUESTIONS

"He's hiding something, isn't he? What do you think?" she asked McKenzie, as they conferred outside of the interview room.

He nodded. "I'd say so. He looked uncomfortable with your questions, Yvonne. I have to say, I'm impressed. I think that posh accent of yours makes them all the more powerful."

She grinned. "Thanks, I think. The problem is, we won't get much more today. His solicitor can't be here for a couple of days, and I have the feeling that lawyer will keep closing us down."

"I agree. Frasier's just admitted to us, however, that he doesn't have an alibi for the time Mack was killed. He also misled us over the time he left the party. I think he has to be at the top of our suspect list."

∼

"Did Macpherson's BMW yield anything?" Yvonne sipped her machine coffee.

McKenzie shook his head. "Nothing useful. It was clean. Only his fingerprints, a few OS maps, and a half-eaten pack of chocolate biscuits in the glove compartment. Besides those, a small toolkit, a spare jacket, and his overnight bag."

"What was in the bag?"

"A change of clothes, and his washbag. That's it. The car is still in the pound, but it's clean."

Yvonne sighed. "I see."

"Helen McAllister chased up the hotel that Mack was staying in that night, and they confirmed he hadn't contacted them since making the booking. We double-checked the credit card details, and it was definitely Mack's card."

"So, why did he park at the loch?"

"St. Margaret's?" McKenzie tilted his head. "Well, the only reason I can come up with, is that it's one of the few places to park for free in Edinburgh."

"It's still a bit of a trek." Yvonne frowned. "And he had to walk from the Royal Mile to the car, collect his overnight things, then trek back to the Royal Mile and his hotel. Doing all that wouldn't make much sense, even if he hadn't intended drinking. I mean, why didn't he simply take his bag with him to the party? He would have had a far shorter walk to his hotel. Are you sure there was nothing else in that bag? Something he wouldn't want his friends to see?"

"I'm sure." McKenzie nodded. "We can retrieve it from evidence for you to go over it again, if you like, but SOCO examined it, and found nothing significant. Perhaps he thought he might fancy a walk to clear his head after a few drinks, so left the car by the loch.You know, work off the alcohol before getting his head down."

Yvonne pulled a face. "We're in the middle of a pandemic..."

"Do you think he was going to meet someone? A prearranged rendezvous?"

She nodded. "That's what my intuition is telling me. Out at the lake, it's peaceful, secluded, no-one to overhear. Perhaps, leaving his car at the loch was the excuse he needed to be out and about for a meeting. If we could find out who he was going to see, we might also find his killer."

"No simple task that." McKenzie rubbed his chin. "But, I like your thinking."

"We should carry on digging among his friends. We still have the birthday boy, Jack Hendry, to interview. We can also continue to rattle the others. One or more of them knows something, Grant."

"And we have a second body. We'd better sort this, or I've a feeling we'll have more."

"Exactly. God only knows how many we could end up with if we don't nail this, and soon."

11

THE POET SPEAKS

Grant McKenzie gathered everyone together in front of the whiteboard in Leith Station MIT. "Right everybody, settle down." He waited for them to fall silent. "I've put up the deciphered message sent to us by the killer calling himself The Poet. You can thank the army for the translation. They came up trumps with the decryption. We have every reason to believe this is from the murderer of Trevor Macpherson and Judge Abernathie, as we haven't yet released any details of the killer's signature to the public. No-one knows about the cocktail stick in the eye, except SOCO, the pathologist, the people in this room, and the writer of this letter."

McKenzie read the translation to the others.

"I'll take their lives
With my knife
Setting free red, red blood
They'll pay their bill
On my hilt
And writhe around in dirt and mud
They will learn

To bite their tongue
Too late to save their skin
I take them down
In blood they drown
Their faces riven
By death's grim grin.
THE POET."

~

"CHARMING." DC Dalgliesh put his hands on his hips, shaking his head.

"Evil." DS McAllister grimaced.

McKenzie nodded. "I think we're all agreed. This is one sick son of a gun. We need him off our streets, ASAP. I'm told this was a fairly simple cipher. The killer clearly meant us to solve it. I'm told, it gave the army decryptors little trouble. He calls himself a poet, but is he? Is he a writer? If he is, is he a member of a writer's group? A poet society? Graham?" he turned to Dalgliesh. "Can you dig into this? Speak to societies, show them a copy of the poem. Ask them if they recognise the writing style? Have they seen poetry similar to this? If so, where? When? Don't give out specifics of the case, just show them the poem."

Dalgliesh nodded. "Okay."

The Scottish DI turned to the psychologist. "Can prepare a profile for us, Tasha?"

She nodded. "I think I have sufficient to go on. I can always change it as additional information comes in."

McKenzie rolled up his shirt sleeves. "Two bodies, one MO and signature. This perp enjoys putting cocktail sticks in dead men's eyes. Why? What does it do for him? Is it a message?" He turned to DC Robertson. "Susan, get on to military police at Faslane. Find out if they had any dealings with Douglas Cameron, the Glasgow publican and friend to Trevor Macpherson. He was a cryptanalyst at the base until five years ago. Did he fall foul of the military police? Verify his reasons for leaving the navy."

"Aye, sir."

"We believe Mack developed an interest in Faslane. What was that interest? Did Judge Abernathie share that interest? Why were they murdered? Did they know each other? When you are talking to those who knew the victims, find out what you can about their connections in the community. Look for links between Mack and the Judge. Show the judge's neighbours Mack's photo, and vice versa. See if they ring any bells with them."

He had a swig of tepid coffee. "What were Judge Abernathie's most recent cases? Could any of them link into the naval base? Or with any of Mack's previous cases? I realise it's a lot of work, but I know you are up to it. Questions?"

Multiple head shakes signalled his team were ready to get on with it.

∽

Jack Hendry arrived for interview dressed in a casual shirt and trousers, over which he wore a short wax jacket.

McKenzie collected him from reception, bringing him to the interview room where Yvonne was mentally preparing herself.

His hair almost white, Hendry stood around five-foot-seven, and portly. The skin flaked on his cheeks as though he had been a while in the sun. He looked about the room, wide-eyed, unsure of where he should go.

Yvonne pulled the chair out for him to sit.

The Scottish DI kicked off the interview. "Mister Hendry, can I call you Jack?"

Hendry nodded.

"You attended a hotel gathering with Trevor Macpherson on the day someone murdered him, is that right?"

"Yes." Hendry nodded.

"And this was to celebrate your birthday?"

"It was my sixtieth, yes." Hendry unzipped his jacket.

"You can take that off, if you want to?"

Hendry did so, draping it over the back of his chair.

"What was the mood like at the party?" Yvonne asked.

"It was all right. Everyone seemed to enjoy themselves. There wasn't any trouble, if that's what you mean?"

"How long were you there for?"

"Let's see, I was the last to arrive. I was told not to get there before three. I was the birthday boy, so they were there with the drink and nibbles, and my birthday cake, before I got there. Prepared the room, you ken. It was all laid out by the time I arrived. I didn't have to lift a finger."

"They rented the room for the occasion?"

"No, it was Douggie's room. He was coming from Glasgow. He rented it so he wouldn't have to travel back afterwards. They decided it would be a as good a place as any to hold the party."

"Had you heard of the Covid rules? Were you aware that you were breaking them?"

"I knew they'd brought in a ban against going to pubs and restaurants in the evening, and I knew that meetings between people from two households is the limit, but we were literally just a day after they brought in the ban, and we'd arranged it months before. Well, not me. I didn't arrange anything, but the others... You ken what I'm saying? We didn't think we'd be doing any harm. And, besides..." He

The Edinburgh Murders

sighed, wringing his hands. "We couldn't have known what would happen to Mack." He shook his head, his eyes on the table between him and the detectives. "You couldn't have wished for a nicer bloke than Mack."

"How long had you known him?" Yvonne tilted her head, her voice soft.

"Since we were bairns in School together. We played for the school football team. He was a striker, I was more a defender. They were good times."

"What do you do for a living?"

"Me? Och, I'm retired. Used to manage a carpet shop until I developed COPD. I took up my pension, such as it was, after the diagnosis. My pension wasnae much. Thank God, for personal independence payments, eh?"

"I'm sorry." She said, voice thick with empathy.

"Och, it's okay. I was more than ready to hang up my boots. You get tired as you age. Things stop working so well as they used to. You become resigned to it. And, the simpler things in life carry more appeal, you ken? Unless, that's just me, eh? My wife still potters about. She gets involved with local events, like jumble sales, and she helps in the local Red Cross shop. I admire her for it, but I prefer my own space."

"How did Mack seem, to you, at the party?"

"He looked like he was enjoying himself. He encouraged me to knock back the beers. By the time my taxi turned up, I was merry as hell."

"Did you see him leave?"

"Aye, I did. He came to hug me and wish me a final happy birthday. He handed me a farewell dram of whiskey. He seemed fine to me. But, like I said, I was a bit the worse for wear, so I could have missed something."

"Was Mack the first to leave?" The DI held her breath.

"No... Er, I think Tom was the first to leave."

"Tom Frasier?"

"Aye, young Tom Frasier."

"Are you sure about that?"

"I'm pretty sure he left first. I'd say, he went roughly half an hour before Mack. Tom didn't say goodbye. That surprised me. I looked at the clock. It was just after nine, but Douggie Cameron slapped me on the back and gave me another dram, asking me to sing with him. I forgot all about Tom sloping off."

"How sure are you about the half-hour you say lapsed between the two of them leaving?"

"Well, Like I told you, I'd had a few bevvies. The time is a rough guess. I didn't check the time Mack left. But I would say it cannae be far wrong."

"I see. What sort of mood was Tom in at the party?"

"I can't say I really noticed. I mean, he was smiling when I saw him, but I cannae say I talked to him that much. I don't know him like I know the others. I knew his dad better. Pete was friendly with Mack, and Mack felt for Tom because his dad died on the oil rig, when he was young."

"Is there anything else you want to tell us about that night, Jack?"

Hendry shook his head.

"Did Mack ever mention Faslane naval base to you? Or show any interest in it?"

Jack shook his head. "I don't recall him ever talking about it, no. I mean, he might have in passing, but nothing stands out. I think most of the guys I know have mentioned it at some point or other, but that doesn't mean they were particularly interested. It's just one of those places in Scotland that people talk about. It's got nuclear submarines. That's what folk usually want to discuss. I know that Douggie there for a while when he was in the navy."

"Did either Mack or Douggie ever discuss that with you?" Yvonne asked.

"I think Douggie might have told us a story or two about his time their. Otherwise, no, they didn't. I don't think there's much else I can tell you, to be honest."

McKenzie nodded. It was clear they had gleaned all they were going to from Hendry at that point.

After they had seen him out, Yvonne reminded Grant that her time in Scotland would soon be at an end.

He jerked his head back. "What? Jeezo, have two weeks gone by already?"

She nodded, placing her hands in the pockets of her trouser suit. "Only a couple of days to go, I'm afraid."

"And you can't extend it, no?"

She sighed. "I don't see how I could. I doubt my DCI would let me have any more time away."

"Well, it's been a real pleasure working with you, Yvonne. You have given me more than a few avenues to explore with this case. You could come again anytime." He smiled, but his eyes challenged her to ask her DCI for an extension.

She understood, knowing only too well how lonely it could feel as the lead investigator on a tough case. The awareness that any decision you make could mean the difference between a killer being locked away, or losing ever more victims. It could be a desolate landscape. Yvonne felt for Grant McKenzie and his team, and couldn't blame them for clutching at anything they thought might help. She, however, had doubts about her own usefulness, not knowing Edinburgh or Scotland very well. That they held her in high esteem was clear, but she felt like telling them she wasn't all that. That she had been lucky more often than she had been right.

Perhaps he understood how she felt. He tilted his head. "You're a far better investigator than you think you are. If you change your mind, we'd be glad to have you back to finish this case with us."

She nodded. "Thank you, I'll remember that. You should find out whether someone saw Mack's car at the loch. If he was due to meet a contact, that person will have hung around there for some time."

12

BAD TIME TO LEAVE

The mist, wrapping around its base, rendered the imposing edifice of Edinburgh Castle timeless.

Yvonne took several snaps with her mobile, persuading Tasha to pose in some of them. "I'm glad I got to see it before I leave," she said, closing her eyes so she might capture the moment in her mind.

She held out a hand to her partner as they approached the monument from the car park in Castle Terrace.

"We could go inside." The psychologist pulled a face. "But Covid restrictions mean some sections are closed to the public." She smiled. "But the up side of that is it's cheaper to get in. Fifteen-fifty a ticket, instead of seventeen-fifty."

"Wow, what a reduction." Yvonne chuckled.

"You know what I mean." Tasha pulled out her tongue. "It all helps. It's all right for you, you're still in receipt of a wage. I'm working this case pro bono, remember?"

The DI took out her purse. "I'm paying for us both."

"Oh no, I didn't mean-"

"I know you didn't." Yvonne took Tasha's arm. "It's the least I can do."

"It's already taken care of." The psychologist grinned, looking pleased with herself.

"What?"

"I had to book online because of the limits on the number of visitors, my darling..." Social distancing and all that.

"Oh, you monkey." Yvonne laughed.

Tasha pulled out the tickets. "I persuaded Grant McKenzie to print these off. I wanted to surprise you."

Before entering the main gate, they took a brief detour to gaze over the wall adjoining the car park.

"Magnificent view." The DI savoured the moment, drinking in the vista of Edinburgh, parts of it covered by the same mist that shrouded the castle. "From up here, you can really appreciate how vast it is."

"It's romantic, isn't it?"

Yvonne nodded. "A view to inspire poetry." Her mind drifted to the case. "Why trek all the way back to St. Margaret's Loch?"

"Sorry?" Tasha raised her brows.

"Mack... I get that he might want to save himself a long-stay parking permit, but it makes no sense to me that he would walk all the way to the loch from the Royal Mile to collect his bag, only to march all the way back to a hotel in the city centre. Why didn't he take his bag with him, and save himself the bother? That would have been the obvious thing to do."

The psychologist nodded. "I think you may be right about him planning to meet someone. I know it wasn't like Mack to make things more complicated than they needed to be. He would more likely take the practical option. No, for whatever reason, he wanted to go to the loch that evening, Yvonne."

"I suggested McKenzie look for witnesses of Mack's BMW at the lake. If he agreed to meet someone, then that person could have been waiting for some time near his car, and may have been seen by others."

"I hope you're right."

"Judge Abernathie could have been about to pass a memory stick to someone before our killer took him out. Could Mack have been doing the same? Passing information, on the night he died?"

"I see what you're saying." Tasha pursed her lips. "And the killer dispatched them both before they could do so."

"Maybe, Tasha, maybe."

They wandered through the gate, handing in the printed tickets to the gloved attendants, who reminded them they must wear face masks inside.

Yvonne frowned. "Tom Frasier knows more than he is letting on, I am sure of it. Remind Grant, when you see him, to lean on the reporter."

"I Will."

∼

TWO DAYS LATER, and Yvonne was back in Newtown CID, being handed a steaming cuppa by her sergeant, Dewi Hughes.

"It's good to have you back, ma'am. We missed you."

"I missed you, too." She took a sip of the hot tea. "How have things been?"

"Hectic." Dewi sighed. "I emailed you a report, to bring you up to speed. Our biggest concern at the moment is the white vans turning up in the villages just before animals and equipment go missing. The villagers are sure that this is not a coincidence. "

"What's being stolen?" The DI frowned.

"Everything from farm machinery, through bikes, sheep, and, the latest craze, defibrillators from outside of the community halls."

"Defibrillators? Why are the criminals after those? There isn't a black market for them, is there? It's worrying if they're taking machines designed to save lives."

Dewi shrugged. "Perhaps they're using them to resuscitate their mates after they've been in a scrum with other gangs."

"A defibrillator doesn't plug the holes left by knives, Dewi."

He grimaced. "I was joking, obviously."

Her face softened. "I'm sorry. I've been feeling tense. It's this case in Scotland."

"How is it going up there?" He took his suit jacket off, placing it over the back of his chair.

"It gets more complicated by the minute. The murders were horrific. The killer sliced up his victims with a zombie knife. There's no doubt murder was the aim, but it's more sadistic than that. It's over the top cruelty, like the deaths are a warning to others. He sent messages taunting the Scottish police and calling himself The Poet. The person responsible is one extremely unhinged individual. At face value, they're dealing with a narcissistic psychopath. But..."

"I get the feeling you think there's more to it?" Dewi leaned towards her.

"There's something more going on."

"Something besides serial murder?"

She nodded. "I'm not convinced they are dealing with a classic serial killer. There have only been two murders so far and, although those killings were horrific and had a clear signature, the victims were criminal justice or ex-criminal justice personnel. There are other niggling details too, like missing data sicks and the odd behaviour of the victims prior to their murders. My gut is telling me these are not random attacks, but targeted slaughter. The question is, why?"

"I'm surprised you walked away from that case, Yvonne." Dewi's eyes scoured her face.

She pursed her lips. "I didn't want to, Dewi, not really. But, I was due back here. I know you guys need me."

Dewi nodded. "Would be good to have your input on the gangs but, once we have that and any instruction you may wish to give us, I could happily run with our cases. If the Scottish team needs your help, then you might be better to give it to them. Hell, they'd be hard-pressed to find another detective with your experience in serial murder. Callum could step up and help me while you're gone."

"You're a good man, Dewi. Where would I be without you?" She smiled. "You are a superb investigator in your own right, and I feel confident enough to leave things in your capable hands. But I doubt the DCI would allow me to extend my time in Edinburgh."

Dewi tilted his head. "You don't know unless you ask."

"Have you any idea where those vans are coming from, Dewi? Do we have registrations? CCTV?"

Dewi noted the deft change of subject. He understood. "One is a Manchester reg. That makes sense, it wouldn't be the first time guys from the big cities foraged over our border. They see this area as a soft target."

Yvonne frowned. "What about traffic patrols? I thought they were hot on this stuff, especially since the lockdown restrictions. How are the perps getting through?"

"It's harder to get in at the moment, but it's not impossible."

She nodded. "I guess so. Plus, there is every possibility they are holing up somewhere around here. They may not be crossing the border at all, right now. They could be lying low with their spoils until the Welsh government eases restrictions again, then hightail it back to England with their haul. Chase it up with traffic. Let them know what they're looking out for. Let's make sure this part of Wales is not an easy option for the gangs."

"Will do."

"In the meantime, maybe uniform could campaign with community councils, and via websites, reminding people to secure their sheds and animals."

"That is not a guarantee of protection, either, Yvonne. They have been cutting the sides of vans like cans of sardines so they can get to the stuff inside them. It's the same with sheds. We have also had a worrying escalation recently. A gang in balaclavas forced their way into an elderly couple's home, whilst they were in the house, frightening the life out of them. The elderly gentleman was beaten quite badly, and ended up in hospital. The gangs are prepared to use violence to get what they want. Our communities are on edge, and the criminals have become emboldened. They tried taking a child off the street in front of her mother, just before we went into the two-week lockdown. This isn't going to end well."

"All the more reason for me to be here, Dewi. I must admit, though, I miss Tasha."

"She stayed up there, then?"

Yvonne nodded. "The killer took the life of her friend. She's there for the duration."

"I can understand that. I hope they find the killer soon."

13

AN ENIGMATIC DEATH

Yvonne had just logged into her emails when DCI Llewelyn came to find her in CID primary office.

"There you are."

"Sorry, sir, I meant to pop in and see you. I've been catching up with the team. I-"

"It's okay." He held up his hand. "That's not why I was trying to find you."

"Oh, okay. Is something wrong?" She stood to meet him.

"I've just had a call from MIT in Edinburgh."

"Have you?" She frowned, her heart thumping. "It's not Tasha. Is she-"

"No, nothing like that. They've had another death, and they think it's related to the case you were helping with. The circumstances are strange, apparently. It's not a straightforward scene, or connection. They have asked me if I would release you, so you can continue working with them. Their SIO is extremely grateful for your input."

"I see." She searched his face. "What did you say?"

He sighed, running a hand through his hair. "I said I couldn't speak for you, and that I would talk to you about it.

Under the circumstances, you could rejoin their team on a secondment, Yvonne, if you want to. I will not direct you to. This has to be your decision, but I will remind you to exercise caution if you do go back. Don't take the case personally, or put yourself in harm's way. Other than that, your are free to go back to Edinburgh if you want to. I would agree to four weeks, initially, extended to six weeks if deemed necessary. I think that should give you ample time to help them move the investigation forward."

"Right."

"Do you need time to think it over? I said I would get back to them this afternoon but, if you need more time-"

"Can I get back to you after lunch, sir?" She scratched her head. "I've a few things I need to get in order."

He nodded. "Of course. I'll speak to you later, Yvonne." He headed for the door, but swung back towards her. "I forgot to say welcome back."

Dewi came to her side, eyebrows raised. "The Yvonne I know would have bitten his hand off."

She sighed. "Under normal circumstances, I would have. I'm concerned about the vans marauding our villages."

"You can leave those to me." He puffed out his chest. "And, if it gets on top of me, I can ask the DCI to pull his finger out."

She laughed, hands on hips. "Oh Dewi, I can always rely on you to cheer me up."

∼

IT DIDN'T TAKE LONG to figure out what she wanted to do.

After giving her DS parting instructions, Yvonne informed Llewelyn that she would rejoin MIT in Edinburgh as soon as practicable.

A brief trip home to pack, and she was on a train destined for Scotland.

Her gaze fell on the social distancing markers in the train's interior. They seemed an evermore permanent feature of life in twenty-twenty. COVID-19 had a lot to answer for, even her disagreement with the stationmaster at Newtown, who had stated that she couldn't buy her ticket on the day, but needed to book in advance. He didn't change his mind until she begged him and, when that failed, pulled out her warrant card, advising him that any delay could cost lives. It wasn't a lie, maybe a minor bending of the truth. That was enough to persuade him to give her the ticket of a passenger who had cancelled his reservation last minute. The only consolation of the restrictions was having a guaranteed seat on the trains in and out of Newtown. They had often been standing-room only. Now at least, things were somewhat more civilised.

~

THE POLICE STATION in Leith thrummed with activity.

"I'm glad you came back." McKenzie handed her several large photographs. "See what you make of these."

The stills were of a man, fully clothed, lying on a bed, his brains blown out by a single gunshot to the forehead. The weapon, a semi-automatic, lay in his right hand.

"Oh..." She recoiled. "That isn't good."

"No." He shook his head. "This is a strange twist, as you will see."

"I'm guessing this isn't the suicide it looks to be?"

He took the photographs from her, spreading them on the table. "We have a white male, clean-cut, wearing a smart suit, with polished shoes, who apparently shot himself in the head with a Browning semi-automatic."

"But you don't believe it's a suicide?"

"He had no wallet, no car keys, and no phone. In fact, no personal items of any kind apart from these..." He showed her another photograph. This time, a closeup of a small jar containing cocktail sticks. "These, and the gun, were the only personal effects."

"Oh God, I get it. We have a death which looks like it's linked to our case. Was it our murderer killing himself out of remorse? I doubt it, it's too neat, and the fact that the victim had no money, keys or mobile, looks more than a little suspicious."

He nodded. "Someone tried to make this look like suicide. And, there is something that makes this even more bizarre..."

"What's that?"

"There wasn't a single label in any of his clothes. Not one garment, not even his pants, had a maker's label. Someone had neatly removed them with scissors. There was, in fact, nothing we could use to identify who the victim was or where he had come from."

"Wow. What about hotel staff? Did he they not have a name and address for him?"

"He gave his name as Frederick Coulter."

"Sounds like a formula one driver."

"He gave a false Edinburgh address. The House doesn't exist. The street is there, but the numbers don't go up that far. So, it's likely the name is also an alias."

"That is odd for a suicide."

"Yes, it is."

"And, I see no powder burns on the head wound," she said, examining the photographs.

"Exactly, and there's more. Someone removed the serial number on the semi-automatic."

"I see." Yvonne frowned. "They etch those serial numbers pretty deep. Removing them isn't easy to do."

"That's right, it's a specialist job."

"Sounds more like an assassination than a suicide."

"Precisely my thoughts, Yvonne. I think someone took this guy out. And that person was a professional hitman."

She peered at the photographs. "It would have been hard to shoot himself to the front of the head because of recoil, and the use of the thumb to pull the trigger. People shoot themselves to the temple, not the forehead."

"Correct. Another reason to suspect this was not self-inflicted."

"What about the cocktail sticks? I'd say they are a coincidence too far. This has to be related to our murders. Do you agree?"

"Absolutely, whoever took this guy out knows about our murderer's signature and must be connected, directly or indirectly, to the deaths of Trevor Macpherson and Judge John Abernathie. If this assassin wasn't our killer, then he was told to leave the cocktail sticks by the person who was."

"The cocktail sticks being another warning to someone, maybe?"

"Perhaps, but we still don't know who the targets are."

"Unless, it's us?" Yvonne frowned.

"The cocktail sticks mean nothing to me."

"Or me," she agreed. "So now, we have a murdered ex-detective, judge, and a bizarre hit on an unknown. What the hell is going on?"

"Whatever it is, Yvonne, it's big. It must be. Someone is going to a lot of trouble, and risk, to silence people. I have a horrible feeling they haven't finished, yet."

14

OFFICIAL SECRETS?

"Looks like intelligence service involvement to me." Tasha peered at the photographs. "Yes, an intelligence service hit."

"Explain?" Yvonne asked her partner.

Grant McKenzie took off his tie, rolling up his shirtsleeves. "Och, I can't wait for this."

"Well, I have only seen one such case before and, I have to admit, I wasn't involved in the investigation. It was a case that occurred in Oslo."

"Okay..." Yvonne leaned in.

"I was at a conference in Düsseldorf, having lectures on how to read various crime scenes in relation to profiling the offenders." Tasha took a sip of water and continued. "One such scene was like this one, in that the deceased appeared to have committed suicide, but someone had removed all the labels in her clothing, the serial number was missing from the weapon, and there were no personal possessions with the body."

"Exactly like our John Doe." McKenzie rubbed his chin.

"Precisely like this, yes." Tasha nodded. "They thought

the victim may have been a member of an intelligence service but, to this day, she remains unidentified as far as law enforcement is concerned."

"Well, I wasn't expecting that." Yvonne folded her arms, a frown lining her forehead. "This case just gets more and more strange."

Tasha pursed her lips. "Just because this looks like an intelligence service assassination, doesn't mean it is. It could be a murder by someone familiar with their methods."

"How do we find out if an intelligence agency did this? I mean, We can't just ask them. They won't admit it to us, will they?" Yvonne sighed.

McKenzie shook his head. "Our best chance for finding out, is to identify our John Doe. If we can find out who he is, and what he was up to, we may also discover the link to our two other victims."

Yvonne nodded. "Makes sense. Why do I feel like we are heading down a very dangerous rabbit hole?"

Tasha grimaced. "Because, we likely are."

Grant's team had posted notices around St. Margaret's Loch and other tourist sites in Edinburgh, requesting members of the public come forward if they had witnessed Trevor Macpherson's black BMW at the loch, on the night he died. The notices also asked if they had witnessed anyone hanging around the area close to the vehicle.

So far, no-one had answered the call, but they believed there was still hope as it was relatively early days.

Four weeks after Mack's murder, McKenzie gave the morning briefing. "We have identified the print on Mack's cheek as that of Douglas Cameron. All points on the partial match. We don't have enough ridges to use as evidence for a conviction, especially since he has already admitted to hugging the victim. But, I think we can be fairly certain it is his print."

"The Glaswegian publican?" Yvonne frowned, aware that Cameron was also an ex-naval employee who had spent time at Faslane's naval base.

"That's the one." McKenzie nodded. "The thing is, because Douggie told us he hugged Mack, and he left the party after the ex-detective, we are not any further forward. Cameron is unlikely to be our killer."

"Unless Mack hung around after the party. Perhaps, to speak with Cameron. I don't think, just because the publican left after Mack, that we can rule him out of the murder." She pursed her lips.

"I agree but, like I said, we would have a hard time proving anything unless we could find a witness who saw them together."

"Just a thought..." Susan Robertson folded her arms. "People don't put their thumb on someone's cheek, when they have given them a hug?"

"If he did hug him." Yvonne raised a brow. "I mean, we only have Douglas Cameron's word for that."

Graham Dalgliesh nodded. "They shouldn't have been hugging at all."

"Hmm." McKenzie nodded. "I agree, you wouldn't normally put your thumb in someone's face when you hug them, but we know these men were heavily under the influence of alcohol, and they were already breaking Covid rules. I don't think hugging was going to give them any pangs of conscience, do you?"

"We don't yet have an identity for our John Doe." McKenzie sighed, hands on hips. "But we know he was exceptionally well-presented, at least until he had his head blown off. We-"

DC Dalgliesh interrupted. "Sir, we've had a description of someone hanging around Mack's car at the lake. The caller alleged a man was pacing around at nine-forty, looking as though he was waiting for someone. Our informant said he was out walking his dog up towards Arthur's Seat. He claims the man was still there when he walked back, at just after ten-fifteen."

"Great." McKenzie ran a hand through his hair. "Do we have a description of the man?"

Dalgliesh read from his notebook. "Six-foot, lean, muscular, light brown hair, he thinks. The man was wearing a red ski jacket. That's all he gave me."

McKenzie frowned. "That could be-"

"Tom Frasier," Yvonne finished for him.

"Yes, Frasier. We know he had a red jacket at the party."

She pursed her lips. "He must have been waiting for Mack, not knowing that he was busy being murdered in Reid's Close."

The psychologist flinched.

Yvonne put a hand to her mouth. "God, I'm sorry, Tasha. That was insensitive. Please, forgive me."

Tasha sighed. "It's okay, carry on with your thread."

"Well, I was going to suggest that Frasier couldn't have been Mack's killer, if he was waiting for him by the car. The description fits, but it's important we verify that information before questioning Tom. Can we show the witness photographs and see if he picks the reporter out?"

MacKenzie nodded to Dalgliesh. "Are you okay to chase that up for us? Also, set up another interview with Frasier?"

"I'll get on it." Dalgliesh disappeared.

"Why was he waiting for Mack?" McKenzie frowned, mulling it over.

"Frasier will have his solicitor with him." Yvonne ran a

hand through her hair. "It won't stop me leaning on him, but I don't think we should let him know he is not a suspect for the murder, even if we confirm he was the person waiting by Mack's car. If he thinks he is under suspicion, he may be more likely to tell us what he knows. I am sure he has more information than he's giving us. He's a reporter. If anyone can tell us the link between Mack and Abernathie, I'd say it's him. Perhaps Frasier was going to give Mack information that night, or vice versa."

The psychologist was deep in thought.

"Are you okay, Tasha?" Yvonne asked.

"I think you should have Frasier watched. If Mack and Frasier *were* exchanging information, then the journalist may be on the hit list, too. In fact, if I may be so bold, I would suggest coming at it from that angle. I think you are much more likely to get the information out of him, if he thinks his life is in danger. The killer may think Mack and Frasier talked about whatever secret he wants to keep hidden. They were at the party together. Information could have changed hands."

Yvonne nodded. "Which begs the question, why wouldn't Mack and Frasier talk at the birthday do, given the opportunity?"

Tasha shrugged. "They may have considered it too dangerous, either for themselves or the others who were there."

"My God, what kind of secret could we be talking about, here? The sooner we talk to that journalist again, the better."

∽

The Edinburgh Murders 95

FRASIER ATTENDED WITH HIS SOLICITOR, Paul Connor, a bespectacled man in his fifties, who trundled his bag on a trolley which was almost as big as he was.

The journalist, dressed in a denim shirt with the sleeves rolled up, kept his arms folded, facial muscles stiff.

Yvonne opened the session. A sore throat gave her a husky voice. "We appreciate you coming in to answer questions, Tom. I'll tell you right away that a witness has positively identified you as someone hanging around Trevor Macpherson's car, on the night he died. They place you at St. Margaret's Loch between nine-thirty and ten-fifteen. They picked your photograph out from a bunch of others. Can you tell me what you were doing at the loch?"

He sighed. "The fact someone selected my photo is not proof that I was at the loch. Witnesses make false identifications all the time. Memory is fallible, and so is the eye. These are both well-known facts."

She nodded. "I accept observers get things wrong. The problem we face, however, is that the killer may believe them. If Mack's murderer hears you were at the loch that night, possibly rendezvousing with the former detective, you yourself could become a target."

"What do you mean?" His wide eyes locked on hers. He took a sip of water. The cup shook.

She cleared her throat. "We think they killed Mack because of something he knew. Perhaps, the information you wanted from him. Or was it the other way around? Did you give Mack information that got him killed?"

"No... Of course not." He shifted in his seat, his gaze falling to the backs of his hands. "That can't be the reason... It just can't."

"You don't sound sure, Tom. I think you know why Mack

was killed. That is why you closed down the last interview we conducted with you. I believe you're scared."

"I'm not afraid." He swallowed hard.

"You know there was a second victim? After Mack? Of course you know, you're a journalist. The second victim was a judge."

"I'm sorry, I have to stop you there." Frasier's solicitor puffed out his chest, the buttons on the front of his waistcoat under strain, the top of his head shining in the glare of the lights. "I can't stand by and watch you attempt to frighten my client."

"How am I frightening him?" She leaned back in her chair. "I'm merely outlining the facts, Mr Connor. Things I believe Mr Frasier ought to be aware of. It would be remiss of me if, suspecting he could be a target for a vicious killer, I failed to notify him of that fact."

The solicitor fell silent.

"Come on, Tom. Give us something to work with."

Tom bit his lip, scratching the stubble on his chin. "Can you protect me?"

"That depends on the information you have, and whether you would comply with any measures, we put in place. If you qualify for witness protection, you'll have all the safety we can offer you."

"The problem is..." Frasier sighed. "I don't have names. I can't tell you who killed Mack, or Judge Abernathie, because I don't know. I can give you the information I have, but it's limited, I'm afraid."

"Try us," she said, her gaze steady.

"I've been working on a story. I have been for some time. It's about missing munitions, the black market trade in stolen weaponry, and internet sales of equipment and munitions stolen from the British army."

The Edinburgh Murders

"Really?" The DI frowned. "How does that relate to the murders?"

"Mack had information for me. The night they killed him, he was going to tell me what he knew. He said the information could be dangerous for me. There are bad actors, who do not want their activities or their networks exposed. They steal illegal weapons from bases all over the globe and sell them on to the highest bidders. They will stop at nothing to keep their black market trade going, there is so much money involved. I became interested because they often use the munitions in attacks on soft targets."

"Did your investigations involve Faslane?"

"Faslane?" He cleared his throat.

"Mack had aerial photographs and plans of Faslane naval base on the desk in his flat."

Frasier rubbed his forehead. "Perhaps, he had information for me about the base."

"Are you telling me you didn't know he was going to talk to you about it? That you didn't know what the information was?"

"I didn't know the specifics. He said it was important, and that people should know, but he didn't tell me what he had discovered, not even the subject. He seemed nervous of emailing, as though he felt he was being watched. Mack told me that what he had was important for my story, and that the information needed to get out."

McKenzie leaned in. "Did he mention Judge Abernathie to you?"

Frasier lifted his eyes to the ceiling, swallowing hard. "No."

"Are you sure?" Yvonne asked.

"I saw his name in the paper." He let out a shuddering

sigh, adjusting the collar on his shirt. "They killed him in the same way as Mack, didn't they?"

She nodded. "Yes, they did."

He pursed his lips, running a hand through his hair. "You think they'll come for me?"

"Who? Who will come for you, Tom?"

"The killers?"

"Well, I guess that depends on what you know, and whether you help us get the bad guys off the streets by giving us the information you have. Do the killers know you about you, Tom?"

He shook his head. "I don't know... Maybe."

She tilted her head. "You could share the burden. Once the information is out in the open, there won't be the same need to silence you, will there?"

"You don't know these people like I do. They're capable of anything."

"Are they arms dealers, Tom?"

"Oh, they wouldn't stop there."

"Are you saying they use them themselves?"

Frasier fell silent.

"Tom?"

He sat with his arms folded, his eyes on the desk.

"How did you get into this? I mean, researching this story?"

He levelled his gaze at her. It was several seconds before he spoke. "Do you remember that plane that disappeared after taking off from Kuala Lumpur airport? Think twenty-fourteen," he instructed.

"Vaguely, I can't remember the details. Didn't it end up in the Southern Indian Ocean?"

He nodded. "Allegedly."

"What about it?" She frowned. "How does that fit in?"

"It doesn't but, at the time it disappeared, the story fascinated me. I followed it religiously for a while. There were hundred's of people from all over the world speculating about the disappearance and discussing it on Twitter."

"Okay..."

"Well, back in twenty-seventeen, someone tweeted that four mini-nukes had gone missing from the UK. I didn't know if this was true, or what the circumstances might have been that led to such weapons being stolen. They suggested it was from a submarine. It could have been total nonsense, but I looked into it. One thing led to another, and I ended up looking into a plethora of stories of missing munitions and who might steal them from the army."

"The British army?"

"Oh, we're not alone. These thefts go on from bases all over the world. The more you look into it, the more frightening it becomes. There are some dark actors involved in much of it. In others, it's a few rogues looking at making a few quid on the internet. For the bigger players, colossal sums of money change hands."

"Were yourself or Mack looking into specific individuals in connection with theft?"

Frasier glanced at his watch, then at his solicitor. "I've got a doctor's appointment this afternoon. I really ought to go."

"Are you going to answer the question?"

"I told you, I have no names to give you." He delivered the statement without emotion. The shutters were down.

Yvonne glanced at McKenzie, who nodded.

"You are free to go," Yvonne advised, as the Scottish detective handed Frasier his card.

"But this is our number. Call it if you have more information for us. I'd advise you to keep to the lockdown rules and keep your windows and doors secure. We'll advise uniformed patrols to go past your house regularly. We can have officers to you in a hurry if there is trouble."

Frasier hesitated, as though he might say more. He didn't. Instead, he sighed and grabbed his jacket. "I'll be in touch." He tossed the words over his shoulder as he held the door open for his solicitor and the bag trolley.

"What do you make of that?" McKenzie asked after they left.

"Talk about a Pandora's box." Yvonne grimaced. "What on earth have we got going on?"

"Do you think he knows more than he is saying?"

Yvonne scratched her head. "He was nervous. I believe he is genuinely fearful of what he has got into. And, what was that about missing munitions from a sub? Could this relate to anything happening at Faslane? Or did Mack suspect something like that was going on, and he got himself into deep water by investigating it? Maybe he was looking at visitors to the base?"

McKenzie exhaled. "We won't understand any of it unless Tom Frasier comes clean with what he knows. In the meantime, I could get onto the military police at the base, see if they can shed any light."

Yvonne pursed her lips. "He's scared. Eventually he's going to spill everything to us. The anxiety will get the better of him. Fear will loosen his tongue. He knows we can't protect him properly until we know what the danger is."

"He's a journalist, Yvonne. He'll be used to putting himself in harm's way in order to get the scoop."

"I know, but this is no ordinary story, Grant. That is clear from the bodies lying cold in the mortuary."

McKenzie nodded. "This is a crap fest. A hot mess. Three

deaths, and things look ever murkier. God only knows where this is leading."

"Have SOCO got anything for us other than Cameron's partial print? DNA? Ballistics on the gun?"

"We're waiting on ballistics. They ruled out the size eight trainer prints. They belonged to the neighbour, apparently. No perpetrator DNA, as yet."

"And we don't have the weapon that dispatched Mack?"

"No, but they have confirmed that the same, or similar, was used on Judge Abernathie. I think we knew it would be."

"What about Abernathie's laptop and phone?"

"Clean. He'd deleted everything before he died. He wiped some files minutes before he left the house. SCD are doing fancy work with the hard drives to see what they can recover. Don't hold your breath, though. The judge seemed to know what he was doing."

"I don't think there is anywhere else quite like it in the whole of Scotland. Or, even, in the UK."

"I need this." The DI held her arms out, taking several deep breaths of the cold air until her lungs felt numb. "A balm for my overheated brain."

"Is the case driving you mad?" The psychologist tilted her head, loosening the zip on her raincoat to cool off a little while surveying the DI.

"It is, Tasha. I think your friend Mack got himself into something bigger and darker than he realised."

Tasha shook her head. "If I knew Mack, I'd say he would have known exactly what he was getting himself into, and would have done it, anyway."

"Even risking his life?"

"Yes, if he thought it important enough." The psychologist cast her eyes over a city far quieter than usual as the pandemic entered its second wave. "You know, I've been thinking. Mack wasn't the sort to flout rules, Yvonne. He wasn't a maverick. I can't get my head around his agreeing to go to a gathering, even a birthday do, if he was breaking the law or putting others at risk. The man I knew wouldn't want to cause the local police any bother. He just wouldn't do it. More likely, he would video chat his friends, and agree to catching up once they lifted the restrictions. What he did the night he died was totally out of character."

Yvonne narrowed her eyes. "He didn't go along with it, Tasha. According to at least one of his friends, it was his idea."

"I know." Tasha blew air through pursed lips, shaking her head. "I don't get it."

"Unless..."

"What?"

"He wanted to see those specific friends for a reason.

Something of such importance, it overrode his sensibilities over Covid."

"Do you mean besides wanting to meet with Tom Frasier?"

"It wouldn't have been that. He could have met with Frasier, one-on-one, without flouting rules or risking infection." The DI folded her arms. "If he had wanted only to meet the reporter, he could have done so without involving his other buddies. No, he wanted to see someone other than Frasier. Maybe he sought to get one of the other men drunk because he required information."

"Which would have been why he was encouraging them all to drink more..." Tasha's mouth dropped open. "Of course, that would make sense. He was prodding someone."

Yvonne nodded. "Or challenging them about something? The question is, who? And why?"

"Do you think one of them may be The Poet?"

"I don't know." The DI's gaze wandered over the city as the streetlights came on. "But I think anything is possible with this strange case. If The Poet is one of them, he wasn't acting alone. The timelines they have given us for that evening are a crock."

"I agree." Tasha nodded. "Shall we head back down? It's getting dark." She reached for Yvonne's hand.

The DI smiled, entwining her fingers in her partner's. "Yes, let's go."

∼

THE FOLLOWING MORNING, Yvonne caught up with Grant McKenzie in Leith Station

"Any news on the identity of our John Doe?"

He shook his head. "Aside from the false name and identity, we have nothing on him. DNA and fingerprints not yielding anything, either. The address he gave was a West-Lothian address, but the street numbers don't go high enough. This man, for all intents and purposes, never existed."

"Except he's lying on a slab in the mortuary." She sighed. "How can a life can be worth so little? It beggars belief."

"Well, we're not giving up on him. Someone killed him, and we are going to find out who, and why."

"Yes, we are," she agreed. "What about missing persons? Have we checked all the lists? Contacted the charities?"

"Nothing has come up so far. We can open it out. Do a national appeal and hope it kicks up something. We can let MI5 and the Serious Crime Squad over the border know about him. You know, he could be an overseas agent."

"Do you think the intelligence services would own up, if he was one of theirs?"

"We'll let them know we have this unidentified body. It's up to them what they do with the information. Perhaps he was on an operation they can't associate with, officially. Either way, it won't stop us doing our best to find out who he was. I feel we owe him that much."

"If we go national, and they want it hushed up, they have to speak to us, surely?"

He shrugged. "Who knows? I've never dealt with a case like this before."

Yvonne perched on the edge of a desk. "I've been thinking about the timelines for the evening of Mack's death, given to us by the friends at the party."

"And?"

"Well, they don't line up. The estimates differ wildly between the individuals."

"Well, they were quite drunk."

"They were, but I think Mack may have had an ulterior motive for bringing them all together and getting them intoxicated."

"You think he wanted something from them?"

"He may have been after information, hoping something would slip."

"You mean, from someone other than his godson, Tom Frasier?"

"Yes, Douggie Cameron would be an obvious one. Ex-navy and previously based at Faslane. We think Mack was showing an interest in that base. An obvious person for him to talk to would have been Cameron."

"And, he'd know the layout of the base and, perhaps, still have contacts there?"

"Right, and he was a cryptanalyst. He could have been responsible for the cipher, or he could have been the intended recipient of the cipher."

"But the killer sent the code to us."

"I wonder..." She held her chin, eyes seeing into space.

"What are you thinking?"

"I'm wondering if the murderer also sent the ex-naval man a copy of the coded poem. A warning to him."

"The poet warning Cameron about talking?"

"It is possible, isn't it?"

"But why send it to us?"

"Perhaps, to send the message he's untouchable? The Poet isn't afraid of us, but Cameron should be afraid of him."

"But the killer couldn't be sure that we would make the cipher public. How would he guarantee Cameron saw it?"

"Well, like I said, by sending it to him. I think we should ask Cameron if he has received a copy."

"And what if Cameron is our killer?"

"Then, we spook him. Ask awkward questions. Put him

under pressure because of his previous connection to Faslane. Let him know we think Mack was looking into something that happened there."

"You really think Cameron knows more than he is letting on?" McKenzie scratched his head.

"I think The Poet was warning Cameron to keep quiet, or keep his nose out."

"Okay, let's get him in again. We'll show him the cipher and the translation and watch for his reaction."

Yvonne nodded. "I believe it's worth a try."

16

A KILLER'S WARNING

"I don't know what you want me to say." Douglas Cameron pushed the cipher away, sitting back in his chair, and folding his arms. "I've never seen it before, and I didn't create it."

Yvonne was sure his cheeks had paled. "Could this have been a coded message to you?"

"Why would it be for me? Why would the murderer of one of my friends send me a cipher?"

"Because he knew you could decrypt it."

"But he sent this to you." He fixed her with an icy stare.

She resisted a shudder. "Did you receive a copy, Mister Cameron?"

He placed his hands behind his head, leaning back in the chair, lips tight closed.

"Douggie?" Her voice was almost a whisper. "This reads like a veiled threat to me. He's talking about the murders he committed, but it seems like a warning to others, telling them to keep quiet or they will suffer the same fate. Don't you think?"

"Why would Mack's killer want to threaten me?"

"Because of something you know."

He shrugged.

"Did you receive a copy of the cipher?"

"No, I didn't."

She could tell he was mulling over her words. He sighed several times in the ten-second pause that followed, shifting in his seat, sweat developing on his upper lip. "Can I go? I don't have what you want." He pushed back his chair.

"What do we want, Douggie?"

"Information, and you think I can provide it. I can't. That's all I have to say."

"Okay." McKenzie stood. "But just you have a wee think about what we've discussed today. The people who killed your friend, and wrote this code, are not messing about. They already have a river of blood on their hands. They're hardly going to quibble over more. I'm sure you want Mack's murder solved every bit as much as we do."

"Of course I do." Cameron scowled. "But, I had nothing to do with it."

∽

"That was a genius stroke." Tasha placed her hands on her hips.

"What was?" Yvonne raised her eyebrows.

"Asking Cameron if he'd received a copy of the cipher."

"Oh, thanks. You got a good look at him from the obs room, what did you think?"

Tasha scratched her head. "I would say, given his body language and reactions, that the killer sent him a copy of the code. He doesn't want to talk, though, does he?"

The DI shook her head. "It's a lot like pulling teeth, Tasha. I'm sure it doesn't need to be this difficult. He's hiding something. I just can't decide whether it is out of guilt, fear, or both."

"If Mack's killer meant that cipher for Cameron, the question is, why send a copy to the police?"

"I have been pondering that, too. Maybe, the perps want us to waste our efforts looking for a narcissistic serial killer when, in fact, they are black market racketeers covering their tracks."

"If this is about the black market, we would have to be talking serious merchandise and enormous sums of money, to be worth all this trouble and death."

"Dangerous, too, if we are talking trade in munitions. Especially if they are as devastating as mini nukes."

"You don't think they seriously have those, do you?" Tasha's jaw dropped.

"I doubt it." Yvonne rubbed her cheek. "At least, I hope that is not what we are dealing with. It was just that Tom Frasier talked about mini-nuclear devices supposedly going missing several years ago. You know, when he said they stole four from a British sub. I have no idea if that is true, but it would be a nightmare situation, if it was."

The psychologist turned her gaze to the window. "Yes, it doesn't sound good." After thinking for a moment, her eyes returned to Yvonne. "What are mini nukes, anyway?"

The DI sighed. "My knowledge about such things is limited, Tasha. But, as I understand it, they are nuclear devices designed for carrying in rucksacks. They pack a much smaller punch than the larger nuclear weapons, but are way more powerful than conventional bombs. I thought we had banned their use and proliferation under the various nuclear weapons treaties, but I am no expert."

"I don't like the sound of those."

Yvonne shook her head. "Neither do I, Tasha. Neither do I."

17

DEVIL'S TRADE

A fine drizzle greyed the air around Crammond, a village on the River Almond, and a suburb in the north-west of Edinburgh. It surrounded the beach with a murky haze, dampening the sand, and blurring the whitewashed houses in the peripheral vision of the man who stood with his face to the skin-numbing wind.

In the distance, a gas flare from an oil rig in the Firth of Forth penetrated the gloom.

Douglas Cameron turned the collar up on his overcoat, buttoning the front to keep out the cold as he stepped out onto the causeway.

A black attaché case burned in his hand, and would do until he could finally offload it. Get rid. Perhaps when he did, the painful churning in his stomach would finally cease. Maybe tonight, he would get the sleep he craved.

"You got them, then?"

The familiar voice had him spinning round, heart thudding in his chest. "Yes, I have them."

"And the unlocked, unmanned doors?"

"I have marked them on the plans."

"And what about the trucks?"

Cameron cleared his throat, casting furtive eyes around the harbour. "The trucks will wait a mile away. I've shown their positions on the map. They won't be there for the long. If the men don't get to them in time, they'll lose their transport."

"They better not..."

Cameron shrugged, swallowing hard. "It's not down to me. I'm just passing on the information. I want nothing more to do with this."

"Or what?"

"Or I'll go to the authorities." Cameron's gaze fell to his feet. "I've had enough."

"You would be ill-advised to talk to anyone else. You know what happens to those who chatter."

"How can you be complicit in the deaths of your friends?" Cameron spat the words. "What kind of monster are you?"

"Don't talk to me about collusion. Your hands are just as dirty, Douggie, and you know it."

"I'm not like you. I don't want blood money."

"You were okay with it before, what's changed?"

Cameron spat into the water. "You know full well what changed, Michael. They murdered Mack."

"You went into this with your eyes open."

Douggie spun round, his eyes ablaze. "You're a barbarian, and you're in bed with the devil!"

"And you're naïve. Look at you. You're not so innocent. You knew what you were getting involved in, and it was obvious how high the stakes were. I didn't see you backing away."

"You don't understand." Cameron shook his head.

A police siren stopped them dead. They ceased talking. Douggie's hands shook.

The sound warped as the patrol car hurried on.

Cameron let out a gasp.

The other man took a step forward. "You're kidding yourself if you think you can wash your hands of this. None of it would have got off the ground without you. Your as mired in this as the rest of us."

The publican lifted the attaché case, taking his arm back as though about to toss it into the Firth.

"I wouldn't do that."

"I'm not giving it to them."

"They'll kill us both."

Douggie bit his lip, arm raised above his head.

"Don't do anything stupid. Think of your family."

Cameron let out a groan of angst, his knuckles gleamed white as he lowered his arm. His round eyes pricked with tears as he thrust the case towards his nemesis. "You bastard, I hope it sinks you."

The other man tutted. "Come on now, Douggie, that's not nice, is it? In a few months' time, you'll have forgotten all about it."

"I'll never forgive you."

"I'm not asking you to forgive anyone. You just need to keep your mouth shut. You'll find your money in the usual place."

As the other man walked away, Douglas Cameron threw up on the sand.

∼

IF MEN DON'T HEED
 They bleed
 Thick, red, wet
 Made to feel
 Cold, cold, steel,
 Dark urges met
 They can't hide you
 I will find you
 My blade doesn't care
 Walking behind you,
 Growing inside you
 The dark is everywhere.
 THE POET

∽

THE ROOM FELL SILENT.

"Here we go again." McKenzie walked over to the whiteboard, facing his team, hands thrust deep in his pockets. "The translation of this one was relatively easy. He used the same method of encryption and didn't vary it."

"He's thumbing his nose at us." Graham Dalgliesh threw his pen onto the notepad in front of him. "He thinks he's untouchable."

McKenzie sighed. "He appears to be growing in confidence. Any luck with poet's societies?"

Dalgliesh shook his head. "Nothing. None of them recognised the poem or the writing style. One or two made suggestions. I checked them out. Not one name given could be our perp."

"Whoever The Poet is, he's not that good." Yvonne called from the back.

"Meaning?" McKenzie tilted his head.

"Well, I'm no expert, but the poetry itself seems pretty basic. I mean, there's no fancy footwork in the language. The fact he calls himself a poet, doesn't guarantee he is one."

"Sure." McKenzie nodded. "But, something leads him to use the literary reference. I mean, why The Poet? Why not The Assassin?"

Tasha cleared her throat. "It could be a hint as to his profession. He could be a writer, or a would-be writer, or he may use words in his day-job. I think referring to himself as a poet will be significant, but Yvonne is probably right, he isn't a professional."

Yvonne stood. "I feel we are being led up the garden path. I hate to think we are wasting time chasing down a psychopath, when this could easily be an attempt to cover tracks by a serious criminal, or criminal gang. Perhaps, we need to get back to the basics here. I think we are all agreed that this poem alludes to people being silenced for what they know or what they could, or have, divulged to others. That being the case, we are not talking about stranger murders here. We know Mack was killed after leaving a party, and I am convinced that someone at that gathering either murdered him themselves, or gave others information about his whereabouts, in order for a third party to carry out the execution. I say we go back to those men and press them harder."

A loud knock had all heads turning to the door.

It was DC Susan Robertson. "Sorry, to disturb you." She looked at McKenzie. "I think you ought to know that the labs have got back to us. They confirmed that Judge Abernathie deleted several messages from his hard drive, which included exchanges with both Trevor Macpherson, and Douglas Cameron. Unfortunately, because of the encryption used, they cannot give us the content of the messages, they can only confirm that communications were sent and received."

McKenzie looked at Yvonne. "We get Cameron back in?"

She nodded. "Most definitely."

18

TRAILS OF THE DEAD

Douglas Cameron attended Leith police station in an open-necked white shirt, black jumper and Jeans. "Can I take this off?" he asked, referring to the pullover.

"Yes, of course..." Yvonne sorted through papers whist she waited for McKenzie to join them.

"Jeezo, I'm sorry. I had a phone call," he apologised as he came rushing through the door, throwing his jacket over the back of the chair next to Yvonne. "Are we ready to start?"

She nodded. "I'm ready."

Cameron leaned back, body language open, breathing steady.

McKenzie gave Yvonne a nod.

She cleared her throat. "Thanks for coming in, Douggie. I'll come straight to the point."

"Okay." He stretched his legs under the table.

"You probably heard that, following the murder of your friend Trevor Macpherson, there was another high-profile murder in Edinburgh." Her eyes scanning his face. "Did you hear about that? The killing of Judge John Abernathie?"

He frowned. "It rings a bell, aye."

"Are you aware they murdered him on the driveway in front of his house?"

"I read something about it, yes." He pulled at his right ear, his gaze levelled at her.

"Did you know Judge Abernathie?"

"Are you asking me if I ever met him?"

"If you had dealings with him, yes." She held his gaze with a steady one of her own.

"I think I may have seen him once. His name rings a bell. Maybe he came into the pub one time."

"Really? Did he drink in Glasgow, then?"

"Well, I only said maybe. His name strikes a chord. I can't picture him, though."

"After he was killed, Douggie, we took his laptop and mobile phone."

"Okay..." He narrowed his eyes, crossing his arms.

"The judge had deleted files, and many of his communications."

"What has that got to do with me?" he asked, raising his shoulders.

"I don't know if you're aware, though I suspect as a former cryptanalyst you would be, but we can find things on hard drives even after someone has tried to delete them."

"I know that." He swallowed.

"We found emails between yourself and Judge Abernathie, and at least one message you had sent to both the judge and Trevor Macpherson."

He coughed, shifting in his seat.

"Do you want to tell us what they were about?"

He chewed his lower lip, sweat clotting the hair at his temples.

"Douggie?"

"I'd rather not go into it." He ran a hand through the damp hair. "Really, I'd rather not."

"I'm not giving you a choice." Yvonne pressed her lips together. "We are looking for their murderer, and you were in communication with them. They had independently erased the three-way communications involving you, and that makes us suspicious. Now, you can wait and have a solicitor with you, or we can get one for you if you prefer. But, whichever way you proceed, we want an answer to the question."

He sighed. "I informed them I was being blackmailed."

"Really?" She frowned. "Who was blackmailing you?"

"Before I tell you, are you going to use the information against me?"

"We can make no promises, Douggie. We are trying to solve two, possibly three, murders. At the moment, you are on the suspect list. We want to know what the connection was between the judge and yourself. Now, you say you told them you were being blackmailed, why did you go to them?"

"They were familiar with the law, and I wanted advice. Mack told me about the judge. He said I could trust him."

"Why was someone blackmailing you? What did they have against you?"

"I sold a few things on the internet."

"What sort of things?"

"Naval equipment." His voice was husky.

"Do you mean equipment from the base?"

"Yes."

"What sort of things are we talking about?"

"Oh, mostly old gear... An old helmet, items of uniform, maps, bits and pieces of ammunition, items I'd picked up on foreign tours, and a couple of pistols."

"Ammunition? Pistols?"

"Only fifty rounds. The point is, I shouldn't have done it, it was stealing from the British navy, and they could prosecute me for it."

She frowned. "Is that really something people could blackmail you with?"

"Well, if convicted, I'd lose my licence to sell alcohol. My publican career would be over and, worst-case scenario, I would go to prison."

"Who was blackmailing you?"

"I can't tell you that."

"Yes, you can."

He hugged himself. "I can't."

She sighed. "If we charge you with murder, and you're convicted by a jury, you can kiss goodbye to the life you have, anyway."

"There's no way you'd get me convicted of murder. You need evidence." He frowned. "And you have very little of that. Deleted messages don't make proof of murder, Inspector. If they did, there would be many innocent people populating our prisons."

"Who are you protecting?"

He didn't answer.

"Are you afraid of someone? Was it more than blackmail? Did they threaten you? Maybe to cut you up?"

"You don't know what you're asking." He spat the words, then sipped from the water cup in front of him. His hand shook.

"Take your time." Her voice was soft. "I think you want to tell us. You spoke to Mack, and to Judge Abernathie. You wanted help. You wanted the threats to stop."

He sipped more water.

"Talk to us. Let us help you."

"He's a friend."

She frowned. "Well, he's not that much of a friend, Douggie. What kind of friend threatens you for money?"

He shook his head. "He didn't want money."

"What then?"

"He wanted information."

"What sort of information?"

Cameron checked his watch. "He wanted plans of the naval base."

"Faslane?"

"Yes, that, and any information I could give him about the running of it."

"Why?"

Cameron shrugged.

"So you approached Mack and John Abernathie?"

"I wanted advice, and to work out my options. I spoke to Mack first. He put me in touch with the judge. I wanted to know where I stood if I resisted the blackmail."

"Did you give them details? Did you tell them that the people threatening you wanted information about the base?"

"I told them some of it, yes."

"Did they report it?"

"I don't know. I asked them not to involve me."

"Who was doing the blackmailing?" McKenzie pushed.

"I-"

"Douggie, who?"

He exhaled. "Mike Muirhouse."

"Muirhouse?" Yvonne scratched her head. "He sells books for a living. What is he doing getting involved in military equipment? Do you think he killed Mack and Abernathie?"

He shook his head. "I don't know."

"Did you tell Muirhouse that you had discussed things with them?"

"He knew I had spoken with Mack."

"How did he know that?"

"He overheard us talking."

"When?"

"The afternoon of the party."

"Was Mack looking into Michael's activities?"

Cameron shrugged. "He could have been."

"What was Muirhouse's demeanour, after he witnessed you and Mack in discussion?"

"Pensive. He was definitely more subdued. He left just after Tom."

"Really?" Yvonne frowned. "Do you know what time he left?"

He shrugged. "It had to have been around nine-thirty."

McKenzie leaned in. "Would you be willing to write a statement, outlining what you have told us. We'll need the dates and times in it."

Douggie swallowed. "If I have to."

∾

AFTER THE INTERVIEW, Yvonne conferred with The Scottish DI. "Muirhouse's bookstore could be a cover for seedier operations."

He nodded. "He could be The Poet."

"I'm having a hard time believing Cameron only sold a few items, though. I mean, I don't see that being a big enough reason for blackmail."

"I agree, I think he's minimising. I bet he was at it for

years before Muirhouse found out, and judging by the fear in him, I'd wager he sold a fair number of firearms."

"I think we should contact military police and find out if Cameron ever got in trouble with them."

"I'll get Dalgliesh on the case. In the meantime, I think we go see Muirhouse. Bring him in. See what he's got to say for himself."

She nodded. "We have enough to arrest for attempted extortion. That's a start."

∼

THE ROYAL MILE was busier than expected. She had left Wales when they had been in a full 'firebreak' lockdown, with barely anyone on the streets. Here in Edinburgh, people were well into Christmas shopping, with barely a month to go.

It was reassuring, seeing a semblance of normality. It wasn't perfect; they had entered tier three restrictions, affecting gatherings, eating and drinking out, and how many households could mix, but it was better than total lockdown, which felt a lot like martial law.

Yellow lines, and painted feet, were constant reminders of Covid, and of the need to keep two metres of social distance from everybody else. But that notwithstanding, at least there was life here. And it went on.

In contrast, Muirhouse Books was quiet. On closer inspection, she could see it was in darkness, the closed sign hanging from the door handle.

"Oh." She glanced at McKenzie. "Is he only open on certain days?"

He peered at the board in the window. "According to

what it says there, the shop should be open. He wasn't answering the phone when we called his home."

"Perhaps, he's ill?"

"Could be... Or busy blackmailing some poor sod."

"Shall we try his house again?" She turned to face him.

"I think we'd better. I'll phone the station and let them know we are heading out there. We may need backup."

∞

MUIRHOUSE LIVED in a Georgian townhouse in Dean Village, on Water of Leith, close to Haymarket station. An affluent area of Edinburgh, it had steep, cobbled streets and houses which harked back to a finer era.

Yvonne was envious. "This place has jumped straight out of a Christmas card. He must have a few bob," she said to McKenzie as they approached Muirhouse's home.

"Aye, it looks a lot more upmarket than I could afford and, I suspect, than could be paid for by owning a bookshop, even one as popular as his."

"I'm inclined to agree." She thumped the lion's head knocker on the front door.

McKenzie jumped over the flower border to peer in through a downstairs window. "I can't see any signs of life in there."

"Me neither." She shook her head. "The place looks empty. I'll give it a harder knock."

No-one answered the door, and there was neither sound nor movement inside.

"It's possible we missed him." McKenzie put his hands on his hips. "If he was late leaving for work or opened later because of an appointment, then its possible we passed each other on the road. He could be at the shop."

Yvonne nodded. "We could try the bookstore again. Perhaps, we should think about obtaining warrants to gain entry."

"Agreed." McKenzie scratched his head. "I'll contact my DCI."

19

THE NIGHTMARE UNFOLDS

Tom Frasier checked his camera and microphone, and that he had fully charged batteries for both. Night vision was on and ready. The human cost of getting this far had been unimaginably high. He couldn't afford to mess this up. He owed Mack that much. The latter had paid with his life. A few hours in the bitter cold were a small price for a journalist to pay.

The drive to Faslane whizzed by. Forty miles from Glasgow took around an hour but, so focussed was he on the task ahead, he couldn't remember much about how he had gone from one place to the next. Miles passed, without him knowing whether he had even kept within speed limits. He hoped there wouldn't be penalty notices dropping through his letter box or, worse, that he wouldn't lose his license through multiple transgressions. Not that any of that mattered. If he got what he came for, it would have been more than worth it.

The mist had thinned but not cleared. Keeping his lens free from condensation would be a challenge. He prayed it wouldn't rain. Rain and mist played havoc with the lighting in his shots.

Cowering in the murk wasn't his favourite thing to do either, but he could comfort himself with being used to it. That he could stay the course, he was sure. That was possibly the only surety he had. The rest was in the hands of providence.

He heard the trucks long before he saw them. He estimated there were two, as he dipped below cover to complete one last check of the settings on his camera.

He captured several multiple-frame shots of the trucks as they rounded the last corner before the base.

The approach roads were long, through grassed and wooded terrain. This was one of the most secure bases on the planet. He knew the vehicles wouldn't get near it without significant help from the inside. He saw his job as helping to identify the traitors.

He knew they would keep at least one vehicle away from the base for an emergency getaway, but Tom was not expecting was for so many bodies to be involved - at least twelve of them in full military fatigues. He sensed something big was about to go down. It was time to get back to the peace camp, and Douggie Cameron.

∼

IT WAS ALMOST five o'clock in the afternoon, when they finally received the warrant to search Michael's home and store.

Muirhouse Books was still in darkness. The closed sign hadn't moved.

McKenzie gave the nod to the uniformed officers waiting to force the entrance.

They did so, announcing they were the police, and shouting for any occupants to show themselves.

There was neither answer nor movement from within.

"Ready?" McKenzie asked her.

"Yes." She followed him in.

McKenzie found the light switch.

"What's that smell?" Yvonne lifted her nose, taking several breaths.

"Something unpleasant." He wrinkled his.

"It's acrid, like..." She strode towards the back of the store, to the last of the alcoves formed by shelved books.

"Blood?" Grant asked from behind.

"Oh, God..." She put a hand to her mouth, stepping back. "We'll need an ambulance and SOCO. This is a crime scene. Someone murdered Muirhouse."

Michael lay where he had fallen, against the wall at the back of the alcove, partially upright. His head had fallen forward over clothing drenched in blood, most of the latter had pooled around him and smeared on the wall above.

Blood had also spattered the books on the shelves, and the floor. Cast-off spray stained the ceiling above.

There was little doubt Michael was dead, but paramedics were on the scene within minutes to confirm it was the case.

Yvonne pressed her lips together.

"Jeezo, I wasn't expecting that." McKenzie suited up to kneel near the body. "They made a mess of him."

Zipping up her own suit, and snapping on two pairs of latex gloves, she joined him. "Looks like he sustained injuries to his back and front."

"Maybe they came at him from behind?"

"He didn't stand a chance." She looked at the bloody

handprint left on three of the books on the shelf to her left. "He tried to get up."

"He was losing a lot of blood. He wasn't going anywhere."

Not for the first time, she wondered what sort of person could do this to another human being. "He's been here a while." She frowned.

"Hence, the smell."

"Maybe twenty-four hours? They probably hit him yesterday, just before closing time."

"Then they coolly hung the sign on the door and locked him in with his own key."

"We should request all local CCTV footage."

"Och, we know one thing at least..." McKenzie sighed.

"What's that?"

"Michael Muirhouse is not our murderer."

She grimaced. "Well, he definitely didn't kill himself, and that's for sure."

"And this brings the tally of dead to four." He stood.

"Do you think he was blackmailing others besides Cameron?"

"Och... Maybe. Are you thinking one of his victims took him out?"

She shook her head. "No, I don't. I think he was murdered for the same reasons Mack and Judge Abernathie were killed. He likely knew too much."

"We should warn Cameron."

"And Tom Frasier." She pursed her lips. "Perhaps we should warn all who were at that party."

∼

"There's something more to this, Douggie. I'm worried this isn't just theft." Tom replaced the lens cap on his camera and slipped it into his bag, sliding down the bank to where Douggie stood on the perimeter of the Peace Camp near the entrance to Faslane naval base.

"What do you mean?" Douggie frowned.

"It feels like an attack to me."

Peace Camp was a small village of brightly painted wooden shacks and caravans, erected in nineteen-eighty-two as a home for those permanently protesting against the country's need for nuclear deterrents such as Trident. Protesters made their presence felt by occasionally forcing warhead conveys to come to a grinding halt on the long roads into the base. The lorries would quickly get moving again, but those involved in the ambush celebrated every minor disruption for the brief victory it was.

"We can't talk here." Douggie pointed to a place further into the trees. "Get your stuff and follow me."

"What's happening?" Tom hissed, his impatience barely contained.

"I don't know." Cameron had his back to the reporter, taking him deeper into cover.

"I won't be able to photograph anything from in here."

"You won't need to." The older man stopped, turning to face Frasier. "But it wasn't safe to talk out there."

"What's going on?"

"They're taking a warhead."

"What? How? They'll never get away with that? That base is way too secure."

"They have inside help."

"I thought so. Why would anyone at the base help them?"

"We're talking enormous sums of money, Tom. Some people will do anything if the pay is high enough."

Frasier gaped at him. "We have to stop them. We've got to phone the police."

"Don't be stupid." Cameron took a step forward. "You won't get your story if the event doesn't go down."

"I don't want the story if that is the price." Frasier swallowed, putting his hands to his head. "I thought I was covering a story about black market trading in stolen naval equipment and small arms, not bloody warheads. For Christ's sake, Cameron, we have to do something."

"It's too late. Whatever is playing out, is going on inside there. There's nothing we can do about it."

"We can get the trade stopped. They can block them getting away with the warhead. We can't just stand here. Where would it end up?"

Cameron shrugged.

"I'm going to phone the police." Tom rooted in his bag for his mobile phone. "You might turn a blind eye, but I can't."

"I wouldn't do that." Cameron's voice took on a harsher tone as he drew himself to his full height, squaring his shoulders.

"I'm sorry, Douggie, but you can't stop me." Frasier began punching numbers.

"Turn it off," Cameron ordered.

Frasier flicked his eyes up, surprised at the cold delivery of the other's words. "I'm not-" He stopped, heart thumping in his chest.

Cameron had a semi-automatic pointed at the reporter's midriff. "Turn it off."

Frasier dropped his phone, raising both hands in the air. "Wait, I-"

"Kick it towards me."

"I-"

"Do it!"

The reported kicked the phone to Cameron's feet.

The latter picked it up and ripped the back off, taking out the battery and sim card. All went into the pocket of his jacket.

"What happens now?" Tom asked, his chest heaving.

"I have to decide what to do with you."

"Wait... Are you a part of this? Is that it? Are you getting a payout? How much are we talking? How many pieces of silver does it take to betray your country?"

"You wouldn't understand. There was a time when I was proud to serve my country."

"Did you sell Mack out? Are you the one who told them where he was."

Cameron smirked. "Told *them* where he was?" He pulled out a hideous-looking zombie knife.

"Oh my God." Frasier's eyes bulged as he recognised the weapon.

"You couldn't leave it alone, could you?" Cameron sneered.

The reported looked around him, head flailing as he sought a way out. "You didn't ask me here to help me get some pictures, did you?"

"You wouldn't make more than a few paces," Cameron warned. "You should have kept your nose out."

"You murdered Mack," Frasier accused him. "You murdered one of your own friends for profit." Tom broke into a run.

Cameron fired his gun.

20

NOWHERE TO RUN

McKenzie's mobile rang. "Yes? What do you mean?" Lines creased his brow. "Jeezo. man. Listen, Graham, we don't want to interfere with anything happening at the base, but get yourselves prepared. Request armed backup to meet us near the peace camp. And inform the naval base. We don't want to interfere with their ongoing operation."

He put his phone away and turned to Yvonne.

"What?"

"Douglas Cameron didn't resign from the navy. They fired him for theft. He got a dishonourable discharge. He also fell under suspicion over a strange death in Cyprus, but they couldn't prove it was him."

She placed her hands on her hips. "He lied to us."

McKenzie nodded. "He did. We've got to get armed units to Faslane," he peeled off his gloves. "And we need to do it in a hurry."

"Why? What's going on?"

"They've declared a major incident inside the compound. It involves the Special Boat Service."

"Wait, we can't have anything to do with that, it's way beyond our remit."

"We're not. Our concern is with what's happening outside of the base. Dalgliesh tells me that Tom Frasier tried making a call to emergency services, but his phone died. The operator thought she heard another male voice in the background. The phone is off, but they've pinged the last known location, and it's near the anti-nuclear settlement at the front of Faslane base."

"Oh no, I bet Tom has been following whatever's going down. He's still after that bloody story."

"Are you ready to go?"

She nodded. "We'll need stab vests and the rest of our gear, if we are heading up there with armed response."

"We can nip back to the station and get what we need." He grabbed her upper arm. "You don't have to go."

"Are you kidding?" She tilted her head. "I haven't come this far to quit now."

"Fair enough..." He nodded. "If you are sure."

She squared her shoulders. "I'm sure."

∽

SHE ADJUSTED HER STAB VEST, tightening the velcro straps before grabbing the handcuffs, spray, and radio left for her by McKenzie. The black earpiece was the last addition, wrapping around her right ear. She turned the radio down whilst they were in still the station.

"I want to go with you." Tasha caught her up. "Please let me come in the car."

Yvonne gave her partner a hug. "We'll be fine, Tasha. I would much prefer you remain here, where I know you are safe."

The Scottish DI appeared in the doorway, a formidable figure in his stab vest, radio turned up so he could hear the chatter. "Armed response and a chopper are on their way. They should be in place by the time we get there. They'll begin an immediate search for Frasier. Nobody has heard from him since the attempted emergency call. We don't know his status."

"Please, Yvonne," Tasha pleaded, her voice cracking. "If they have taken Tom hostage, I could help with negotiations, couldn't I?" The psychologist turned to McKenzie. "You don't know what you're dealing with?"

Grant raised a brow at Yvonne. "She has a point..."

"Don't you start..." Yvonne admonished, turning her attention back to her partner. "Look, Tasha, you're right, we don't yet know what we are dealing with, and that is another reason I feel it would be better if you remained here. You could advise us from the station."

"You know it will be easier if I am there," the psychologist asserted.

Yvonne turned to McKenzie, the mental dissonance obvious in her pained expression.

He held his hands up. "Don't look at me."

She returned her gaze to Tasha. "All right, you can come with us. But, for God's sake, stay with me. Don't be tempted to go after anyone or put yourself in harm's way. We take a back seat and leave this to armed officers, no matter what happens. Is that clear?"

"Of course it is, thank you."

"You'll need this." McKenzie grabbed a spare kevlar vest, handing it to the psychologist.

DC Dalgliesh joined them late, catching up with them at their vehicle. "Sorry, needed to pee," he said, before jumping into the driver's seat of the BMW.

"Let's go." McKenzie took the front passenger position, leaving the two women in the back.

Dalgliesh put his foot down.

∾

TOM COWERED IN THE DARKNESS, left hand holding a gaping wound in his right bicep to stem the bleeding. He grabbed the camping knife from his bag, pulling his shirt out of his jeans to cut a sizeable patch for use as a bandage. After slashing and tearing, he had a piece that would do.

Grimacing, he bit his lip. The slightest movement was agony. He was close to fainting from the pain.

Using his teeth and left hand, he fumbled the bandage around the wound, resisting the urge to cry out as he pulled the knot tight.

He wasn't sure where Cameron was. Tom had carried on running after the bullet tore through his flesh, weaving between the trees, putting enough distance between them to enable him to go to ground. Each footfall pounded painfully through the injured limb, firing off every torturous nerve ending, and causing waves of dizziness and nausea that threatened to make him pass out.

He knew the ex-serviceman was hunting him. The arc of torchlight swung through the trees, not two hundred yards away. He didn't dare stand, preferring to wait until Cameron either gave up or moved on. Thankfully, the older man's fitness had waned in later years. Tom had youth and strength on his side. Even with his injured arm, he prayed it would be enough.

Overhead, he heard the drone of a helicopter, and shouting from somewhere inside the base. He wondered how Cameron could have got himself involved with the gang of criminals causing the disruption. The navy seals would rout them. Of that, he was in no doubt. Pity his own salvation wasn't as assured.

The light from Cameron's torch passed overhead.

Frasier held his breath, shivering, pressing his teeth together to stop them clattering from shock and cold. Hugging himself hurt, but helped him feel smaller.

He pushed his right hand through the gap between two of his shirt buttons, the nearest thing he had to a sling, preparing to move again. The arm, now bandaged and supported, throbbed less but only by degrees.

It was tempting to stand. To get it over with. The fear of death being unbearable. He chided himself for this ridiculous thought. He couldn't give up. Not now.

21

FRAUGHT

It took forty minutes to arrive at the cordons set up by Glasgow Police, on the approach road to the anti-nuclear encampment, outside of Faslane naval base.

They parked the car in a tiny lay-by, walking the last fifty metres to where two armed officers stood guard. The latter held their weapons across their bodies, barrels down, trigger fingers parallel to the bullet chambers, faces hard.

McKenzie strode over to talk to them while Dalgliesh and Tasha waited with Yvonne.

The latter took several deep breaths to calm her thudding heart. A panic attack was the last thing she needed.

She could hear the low drones of helicopters, sure there were at least two. The more distant one hovered over the base, involved in whatever was going on in there. The other was closer, circling above the trees. It had to be theirs. It was looking for Tom.

Onlookers, from the peace camp, stood next to their caravans and shanty houses, trying to see what was going on. One of them, a tall guy with plaited hair, stood barefoot. She wondered at his hardiness in temperatures of minus two centigrade. Another held a video camera, filming everything he could. The result would end up on their YouTube channel and Facebook pages, providing further evidence for followers that having nuclear weapons is inherently dangerous.

Behind the DI, the first ambulance crews arrived.

Icy rain fell. Though intermittent, it had the power to chill a person to the core.

She buttoned her long coat, and thought of the young reporter, wondering where he was. Had he got a jacket? Was he still alive?

McKenzie rejoined them. "They're going to get the onlookers back in their shacks. We can't guarantee their protection if they stay where they are. Not from our killer, or from what may happen at Faslane." He turned his attention to Yvonne. "You're quiet... Are you all right?"

She nodded. "I just hope we find Frasier soon. God only knows what he has got himself into."

"There's not a lot we can do at the moment until the helicopter or the guys on the ground locate him. He's probably somewhere in those woods."

"He hasn't tried calling again." Dalgliesh confirmed, as he ended his call to Leith station. "His phone is still dead, apparently."

Yvonne turned to Tasha. "It isn't looking good, is it?"

Tasha pursed her lips. "It is worrying, but don't give up hope. Frasier could be in hiding and, if the killer is close, he may have felt it safer to switch his phone off."

"Damn it! There's a delay with the dogs..." McKenzie placed his hand on his hips. "And without them, in this weather, it could take ages to locate a body."

Yvonne flinched. "God, I hope that's not what we're going to find... What's the problem with the dogs?"

"The teams are out on other jobs. It's been a night for it." The Scottish DI shook his head. "The world has gone mad."

"Sod's law." Dalgliesh pulled a face.

"Any news on Cameron?" The Scottish DI asked?

"I'm afraid not. Officers went to his home half an hour ago. He wasn't in. His current whereabouts are unknown. They've requested all units keep an eye out. The house is being watched."

"Fine. Keep me informed, will you?"

Dalgliesh nodded. "I'll let you know as soon as I hear anything."

∾

Tom was sure Cameron had turned his torch off. He could no longer see the arc of light sweeping through the trees.

His entire body shook. While the beam was visible, Frasier had known where his nemesis was. Now, he didn't know whether to get up or stay put.

He felt the first tingling patter of rain on his face. Having removed his jacket so he could bandage his arm, he had the difficulty of manoeuvring it back around his shoulders. At least his left arm still worked, even if stiffened by the cold. His right upper arm was numb. This feeling alternated with searing pain that gritted his teeth. If he held the limb in a single position, the discomfort would ease for a few minutes, but the fire always came back. Changing positions gave some relief, but it was short-lived.

Feeling wretched, he considered making a run for it. He risked being shot in the back, but sometimes he thought anything would be better than the spasms in his arm and the spine-chilling cold. Hot tears pricked his eyelids. How much longer could he hold out?

The helicopter having moved further afield; he heard leaves rustling to his left and turned in time to see Cameron coming for him. The publican's torch was on again now the chopper wouldn't spot him.

"Damn it!" Frasier hoisted himself up, running and stumbling tree to tree. The weaving slowed him down, but offered some protection, should Cameron fire his weapon again.

The hunter was gaining ground.

Tom felt the inevitable about to happen. He closed his eyes, steeling himself for the shot and a thud in the back. Weakened by cold and blood loss, he struggled to keep his legs moving. He fell twice. The second time, he struggled to get up. Cameron would be on him within moments. He swung round, anger replacing fear.

"Go on, get it over with," he roared over the beating of the rain. "If it's what you want, go ahead. I'm not running anymore."

Cameron stopped dead, his mouth open in surprise. He raised his gun, then lowered it again. Armed police were close by. He drew the knife instead. "You shouldn't have poked your nose in, Frasier. We weren't harming you. It wasn't any of your business, but you had to get your story."

"You need to take a good hard look at yourself," Frasier spat defiantly. "Use a mirror and see what a traitor looks like. I'm a reporter. Exposing crooks like you is what I do. You don't care how many lives you ruin or where your illegal trade ends up. You're a psychopath. So, go ahead. Kill me, if that's what you intend to do." Frasier closed his eyes, his bottom lip quivering.

The publican took a step forward.

"Armed police! Stay where you are! Armed police!"

The drone from the helicopter was once more overhead. Blinding light flooded the area around the two men.

Cameron lunged for Tom. Grabbing him by both arms, he thrust him towards the advancing officers before taking off through the trees.

Frasier held his good hand in front of his eyes as the beams of several torches shone in his face.

Armed officers continued past the exhausted reporter, while another pulled him to safety.

Tears of relief streamed down Frasier's face. Finally, he was safe.

22

HEAD-TO-HEAD WITH A KILLER

They took Frasier to the back of one of the waiting ambulances, an armed officer handing him over to a male and female paramedic team, who wrapped a foil blanket around his shuddering shoulders.

He sat upright on the trolley, while they inserted a drip and checked his vital signs, before assessing and cleaning the wound ready for the journey to hospital.

Yvonne walked to the open doors and waved to him. It was her way of letting Tom know he hadn't been alone.

He motioned her in.

The male paramedic held his hand up. "Sorry, we need to get him to the hospital."

"No problem." She turned to go.

"Wait, wait, I want to talk to her, please?" Frasier called out, his voice cracking.

The paramedic nodded. "Okay, but we can't be too long."

She sat next to the reporter on the trolley, while the paramedics continued to treat him.

"I told Mack, about the munitions and equipment smuggling. It was my fault he got involved in the investigation. They killed him because of me." He hung his head.

"It wasn't your fault, Tom. You didn't know what would happen. Mack was a seasoned detective. He would have known the risk he ran. You shouldn't blame yourself. Now, get off to hospital. We can talk about this when you're recovered."

"He was a good man, and a father to me after my own passed away. I saw more of him than I ever did of my own dad, who would be away for months on end, out on the rig. That was even before dad had the accident that killed him. I trusted Trevor. I told him what I knew, and he agreed to help me look into the weapons dealing and expose those involved."

"Why didn't either of you speak with Scottish police?"

"Because I wanted to break the story, and... because of Muirhouse."

"Michael Muirhouse?" In her mind's eye she could see the bloodied inside of the bookstore.

"He was Mack's friend, and he'd been my father's best friend. I didn't want police involved until I knew how, and even if, Muirhouse was involved in the what was going on. I couldn't have forgiven myself, if I'd fingered an innocent man. A source at the base told me about Michael. I can't name that source, I hope you understand that."

"Where did Muirhouse fit in?"

"Michael plays the big I am. He boasts about how he has rich and famous clientele - millionaires, billionaires, and celebrities - all asking him to source first edition books for the libraries in their prestigious houses. And, no matter how obscure their request, he gets them what they want. He lives in a swanky home. Everyone believes that books are how he makes his money, but I know different..." Tom fell silent, lost in thought.

"Was he gun running?" Yvonne prompted.

"He has a darker side. Everyone knows he has a temper, and that he can handle himself. He's a regular at the gym and had been an amateur boxer in his youth. But they don't know he is into providing other things for rich bidders, including weapons."

"What sort of weapons are we talking?"

"Pretty much anything he can lay his hands on. My source alleges Michael Muirhouse organises thefts from military bases all over the UK and elsewhere. He is part of a worldwide network of smugglers. The source couldn't report it because Muirhouse has something on him. I haven't discovered what that is. We involved the judge."

"Judge Abernathie?"

Frasier nodded. "It was increasingly obvious that this was not something Mack and myself could handle on our own. Mack suggested we involve Judge Abernathie, who had contacts within the civil service and intelligence. We really did not know how deep this thing went. Mack felt it might require delicate handling, because of the effect it could have on diplomatic relations."

"What do you mean, in what way?"

"Some stolen munitions may have been used in international atrocities. Muirhouse doesn't care who he sells weapons to. So long as they pay up, he isn't fussy."

"Muirhouse is dead."

"He's a... What?"

"He's dead. We found him earlier this evening."

"How?" Frasier shook his head. "I don't understand..." His eyes widened. "Did Cameron finally turn on him?"

"What makes you ask that?" She tilted her head.

"What I didn't know, until today, was..." He sighed. "Muirhouse had involved Douglas Cameron in the smuggling. I should have seen it. He was an obvious link with Faslane. It made sense that Muirhouse would use Douggie in that way. I think Cameron killed Mack and the judge when he realised they were investigating him. I think he worked it out the night of the party. He has a knife, a-"

"Zombie knife?"

"Yes, exactly, a zombie knife." Frasier's eyes widened. "He has a gun too, hence the hole in my arm. Your guys should be careful. I believe he'll do anything to avoid capture. And if Muirhouse is dead, Cameron must be the one responsible."

"We have to go." The male paramedic ushered Yvonne to the open doors.

"Okay." She turned back to the injured Frasier. "Good luck, Tom, get well soon. Officers will be along to take your statement in the next day or two."

"Goodbye, Inspector." Tom gave her a two-lidded wink, his way of thanking her.

As the DI watched the ambulance go, she pondered the things Frasier had told her. They confirmed what she suspected, Douglas Cameron was a ruthless killer.

∽

MULTIPLE ARMED POLICE officers pushed on through driving rain, torches illuminating the ground between the trees.

Cameron stumbled over rocks and forest detritus, using the cover to dodge the advancing officers and the scouring beam from the police helicopter.

Now and then, he would stop, crouching behind a trunk,

waiting for the light from the chopper to pass by. All the while, the shouting came ever nearer.

He came up short at a high, tensile fence, too large to scale. Cameron was trapped.

He fumbled in his pocket for spare magazines for his Browning semi-automatic, reassuring himself they were still there, having already decided he would tough it out. He found himself a decent-sized tree, and squatted behind it, gripping his gun in readiness for whatever came next.

Heavy boots thudded through the undergrowth.

Cameron flicked off the safety.

"Armed police! Come out with your hands up!"

He took a deep breath, his back to the tree.

"Armed police! Come out with your hands up!"

The boots were close now, couldn't be much more than a couple of hundred yards.

He muttered to himself, "One, two, three." And, whipping round to the right, he fired at the advancing officers.

That he hit one of them was clear from the agonised cry. He didn't know where the bullet had impacted. His shot would be unlikely to penetrate a kevlar vest at that distance, so he figured he must have hit him in the arm, leg, or head.

Cameron took a deep breath, whipping round to fire again.

Several shots rang out, none impacting the publican, but several hitting the tree. Splinters sprayed either side of him.

"We have you surrounded! You have nowhere to go. Drop your weapon and come out with your hands up!"

The helicopter hovered directly overhead. The noise drowned out the calls of the advancing police. All around him, leaves kicked up, swirling about in the draughts created by the threshing blades.

He left his cover to shoot again.

A burst of rapid fire rang out. Cameron's body shuddered with the impact of several bullets.

The publican fell to his knees, the semi-automatic falling from his hand.

Several officers ran to his position.

Their antagonist collapsed face down in the mud.

∽

CAMERON WAS BARELY alive when they brought him to the waiting ambulance.

Yvonne watched as the paramedics worked to get him stabilised, so they could safely transport him to hospital. An armed officer accompanied him into the ambulance.

She pressed her lips together. Cameron had given his own victims no such quarter. If he survived long enough, they would take the publican to intensive care, where he would be subject to the best treatment the NHS could give. His victims, conversely, bled out in the street.

"Thank God, they got him." Tasha leaned her chin on the DI's shoulder. "It's finally over, and the rain has stopped."

Yvonne nodded, leaning her weary head against the psychologist's. Clouds of their breath mingled in the air. "I wonder how many others there are like Cameron and Muirhouse, people waiting in the wings to take over their slice of the black market weapons trade?"

Tasha sighed. "Unfortunately, there are many angry people in the world, wanting to force their particular grievances in the faces of others, and prepared to use horrific violence against those they perceive as their enemies. So long as they pay a high price for the means to do that, there will be suppliers like Cameron and Muirhouse. But, this supply chain is off the streets, and that is down to us,

McKenzie's team, my friend Mack, and an honest reporter. I am proud of what we have achieved, Yvonne, and I know Mack is smiling right now. His death wasn't in vain."

The police helicopter flew away, leaving an eerie silence. The chopper over Faslane base had disappeared half an hour before. Events over the fence had come to a swift conclusion.

"You don't mess with the Special Boat Service." McKenzie grinned as he and Dalgliesh rejoined them. "It's a superb result for us, and them. Is everybody all right?"

Yvonne rubbed her eyes, dissipated tension leaving her drained. "I'm just glad it's done, and that we found Tom Frasier alive."

McKenzie nodded, unbuttoning his overcoat, his expression sober. "He was lucky, it could have ended so differently. He should have told us what he knew far sooner than he did. I hope he's learned something from this. Some things are not worth risking your life over, even for a journalistic scoop."

23

THE ANSWER

Two days later, Yvonne and Tasha joined McKenzie and his team for coffee. Trevor Macpherson's funeral was taking place the following day, and the day after, the DI and psychologist would head home to Wales.

Dalgliesh handed McKenzie a steaming mug from the tray he carried, just as the Scottish DI's mouth gaped in a loud yawn. "There you go, strong and black. You look like you could with it today."

"Jeezo, you can say that again, Graham. I'm fair done in."

Yvonne grinned. "You can't take the excitement."

McKenzie raised his brows. "How are you looking so fresh? What's your secret? I could have done with another couple of hours sleep, me."

Yvonne grimaced. "It'll probably hit me later or tomorrow. I think I'm still running on the adrenaline."

"Aye, you'll be glad to be going back to the sedate countryside, I dare say." He took a gulp of his coffee. "Ah, I needed that."

Yvonne laughed. "It's not always that quiet. We have our fair share of horrible crimes, you know. Why, sometimes folk even refuse to give us their name and address," she quipped.

McKenzie chuckled. "Och, you're fast, you."

She laughed. "I have my moments."

DC Helen McAllister and DS Susan Robertson joined them in the meeting room.

DS Robertson grabbed a mug from the tray. "SOCO found screwed up paper in Muirhouse's bin in the shop and, guess what?"

"Go on..." McKenzie put his coffee down.

"Poetry. Or rather, scribbled-out lines of poetry. He was working on it in English, before transcribing it into a cipher."

"We should have looked at him earlier." He sighed.

"There's more. They found code books in the desk in his office."

"So, Cameron was committing the murders, and Muirhouse was covering up?"

Robertson nodded. "And, Operation Cocktail Stick was a mission Cameron had taken part in while in Cyprus. It was during that mission, that one of Cameron's fellow naval officers was murdered. Suspicion fell on him because he was one of the last people to see the victim alive. But they couldn't prove anything. It's now a cold case. I would think, following what's happened here, they will reopen the investigation."

"If he narrowly escaped conviction for a previous murder, why would he allude to that mission in his murder signature?" McKenzie frowned. "Was it a deliberate taunt? Was he saying, I got with it before, I'll get away with it again?"

Yvonne ran a hand through mussed blonde hair. "The cocktail stick was to convince us we were looking for a psychopath selecting victims who were strangers. Muirhouse compounded this with his poetry. I think they came up with the idea together. If Muirhouse was aware of Cameron's involvement in the murder in Cyprus, he may have been blackmailing him to get information about the base. Cameron seemed like a man on the edge when we interviewed him."

"A complicated partnership." Susan Robertson nodded. "Muirhouse's ego stopped him from realising that he was digging his own grave."

Yvonne sipped her coffee. "Frasier said Muirhouse thought himself Mister Big. He believed he was in control. I think Cameron bided his time, playing along until he could take him out."

McKenzie nodded. "Mack, and Judge Abernathie were part of the fallout. They had cottoned on to what was happening, so Cameron took them out, too. Creating the serial killer scenario to get us thinking these were stranger murders."

"Our John Doe was a member of British intelligence. He agreed the meeting with Abernathie via an email stored on the data stick stolen from the judge." Dalgliesh shook his head. "Instead of Abernathie, he got Cameron, and a bullet to the head."

McKenzie raised his coffee mug. "At least we got the bad guys. Well done all of you. This case was far from easy, but we pulled it out of the bag when it mattered. Tom Frasier would be dead if we hadn't got there in time. Cheers."

They clunked their mugs together. Yvonne had finished her drink, but clunked anyway. They had every right to feel proud.

TASHA READ through the eulogy she was to give at Trevor Macpherson's cremation one last time before the taxi dropped them off at the Mortonhall Crematorium. A strikingly modern building, thin slithers of window ran contiguously down each of the geometric towers.

A lone tear wended its way down her cheek, as she turned her gaze to the rain-sodden streets outside.

Yvonne gave the psychologist's hand a gentle squeeze, eliciting a pained smile from her partner. "Are you all right?" she asked, her eyes studying Tasha's ashen face.

"Yes, I'll be fine." The psychologist folded the piece of paper, slipping it inside her clutch bag. "I hope I do him justice, Yvonne."

"You will, I know you will, my darling." The DI gave her a nudge. "You'd better, I'll be streaming live to your colleagues at the Met-"

"Oh, the iPad..." Tasha's eyes widened. "Where-"

"It's okay." Yvonne pointed to her own bag. "I have it. I knew you'd have other things on your mind, so I popped it in with my things. We have all we need."

"What would I do without you?" Tasha asked. "You're my rock."

The DI paid the taxi, and the two made their way to the left of the main building, to the smaller Pentland Chapel.

The oak coffin with brass handles, paid for by Mack's ex-wife, lay on the catafalque, at the front of the chapel, covered in a turquoise velvet cover edged with white frills. Behind it, curtains of the same colour covered the conveyor to the furnace.

There were two television screens available, a free-standing one to their left, and another attached to the wall on their right.

They sat on a pew at the front. Aside from the reverend and organist, they were the only ones there.

Yvonne took out the iPad, opening the Zoom app, and the connection to those at the Met who wanted to be a part of the service but could not because of the English lockdown.

To her surprise, the connection worked first time. She gave those watching a wave, including Mack's ex-wife, who had joined the police team for the screening. The DI signalled to them it was about to start.

At the back of the chapel, someone coughed.

Yvonne turned to see Tom Frasier, dressed in a shirt and black tie, his arm in a sling. He waved, as he could not get closer to them because of social distancing.

Yvonne waved back, pleased that Mack had at least one more person at his funeral.

The pastor said a few generic words, before Tasha replaced him at the small wooden lectern.

She trembled as she opened up the page containing the script she had spent hours pouring over the night before.

Yvonne felt like running to the front and throwing her arms around her partner, arms that were already beginning to ache from holding up the tablet.

Tasha cleared her throat. "I had known Mack for the best part of twenty years. He was there when I took my first foray into criminal psychology in the actual world. I was green, afraid of messing up. He was the one who reassured me that mistakes were okay. That no battle was ever won without casualties. And that was typical of Mack. A man with a big heart, he was there for everybody. And we all knew it. He put others first, always. He died, doing what he loved most, investigating crime for the benefit of past victims, and the prevention of future ones. I last saw him at the meal for his retirement from the Met. He invited me to come up and see him and Edinburgh, this beautiful city, the place he was born and grew up in. I put it off, believing there was plenty of time. I regret that. Our friend was taken too soon, but his legacy lives on. There are many alive today who have him to thank for the breath they take. We all loved Trevor Macpherson, and we will miss him."

Tears fell onto the page, as Tasha folded it, nodding to the pastor, and returning to her seat next to Yvonne.

Yvonne gave her a reassuring smile, holding the tablet up with one hand, while she rubbed Tasha's arm with the other.

They sang the hymn 'Nearer to Thee' as the coffin began its journey through and beyond the curtain.

The DI waited until it disappeared before signing off the connection with the Met, letting them know Tasha would call them later that day. She gave them a wave and logged off the app.

Finally, she could put her arms around her partner.

Tasha leaned her head into the Yvonne's shoulder, letting silent tears fall as they may.

∽

THE FOLLOWING morning dawned cold and clear. Thick layers of hoar frost coated the hills and the branches of trees, while billowing puffs of steam rose sporadically over the city, as the morning commute began for those allowed to work in the current Covid era.

Yvonne woke early, five minutes to six. She opened their bedroom window, in Braid Hills Hotel, Western Edinburgh, to take a lungful of the crisp morning air, closing it again when she became chilly.

"Beautiful," she whispered to herself, feeling a pang of regret that they would be leaving the city the following day.

She turned around to face the still-sleeping Tasha, chocolate curls spilling round her face where the psychologist had allowed her hair to grow.

The DI smiled, thinking how beautiful her partner looked, lost as she was in restful sleep.

Yvonne ordered breakfast with room service, as they planned to spend several hours walking. They had fortuitously picked the perfect day for it. She left the psychologist sleeping and went for a shower.

By the time she returned, Tasha was awake, sitting upright, eyes glazed.

"Penny for them?" Yvonne asked.

"There you are." Tasha smiled. "I wondered where you'd gone. I was just wishing we had a little more time to explore."

Yvonne grinned. "Well, I have ordered our breakfast here, and we're going to walk up past the lochs to Arthur's Seat before heading back to the Royal Mile for lunch. We may have time to do something else in the afternoon. Make a day of it. If we start early enough, it'll seem longer. And, if you like, we can come again for a holiday in the spring or early summer. Spend a couple of weeks here when we are not working a case. What do you think?"

"Can we?" Tasha's eyes lit up. "I would love that. We could really do the city justice if we had two weeks."

The DI nodded. "We could."

A knock on the door interrupted them.

"That will be breakfast." Yvonne opened it.

The waiter stepped back from the trolley, keeping a social distance, whilst they collected their food.

They thanked him, taking their trays to the bed, Tasha in her pyjamas, and the DI in her hotel dressing gown with a towel around her head.

Both having eaten little the previous day, they tucked into the full English, orange juice, and strong coffee, with relish, until the only thing left was a part-eaten slice of toast.

~

LESS THAN AN HOUR later and they were in all weather gear, walking through Edinburgh's Royal Mile, taking in the sights and sounds before heading up towards the lochs and Arthur's Seat.

"I should have done this at least once with Mack." Tasha sighed. "I feel bad that I never made the effort. They always say don't put off till tomorrow what you can do today, and it's true. We should always aim to spend time with those we care about."

Yvonne nodded. "We should, but in the busy day-to-day, it's easier said than done." She paused as they approached St. Margaret's Loch. "That's one thing to be said for this year's lockdown. To an extent, it has helped slow everyone down enough to reconnect with those around them, particularly their families. Time they wouldn't ordinarily get."

Tasha agreed. "How did Kim get along with the children?" she asked.

"Well, last time I spoke to her, they were back in school, but she tells me she's really valued the extra time with them. Its so precious while they are still relatively little."

The psychologist nodded. "I bet they drove her around the twist on occasion." She grinned.

"They did, but that's all part of it, isn't it? I miss them. We must pay a visit when this Covid threat is over."

"We will."

The cliff at Arthur's Seat stood, majestic, in the winter sunlight. Rising as it did, over the city, it felt like the top of the world.

Yvonne grabbed Tasha's hand, running with her towards the top, until they collapsed on the ground, tired and out of puff.

"You've taken leave of your senses." The psychologist laughed. "At this rate, you're going to kill me."

The DI leaned back on her hands, legs stretched out toward the views over Edinburgh. "No, I'm not." She smiled. "I'm going to marry you."

Tasha gaped at her. "You are?"

"Uh huh, I am."

The psychologist swallowed, breaking into a wide grin. "That is fantastic!" She crawled over to her partner. "That just makes everything perfect."

"I thought you'd approve."

Tasha scratched her cheek. "But, what about those who don't know about us yet? Have you stopped worrying about them?"

The DI grabbed her hands. "I should never have worried about them. I love you, Tasha. You are my world. I don't care who knows it, or when they find out about it. So long as you know, and you feel loved, it doesn't matter."

"Are you sure?"

Yvonne pulled her partner to her feet, putting her arms round her waist and her chin on her shoulder, while they gazed out over the city. "My darling, I have never been more sure of anything in my life."

The End.

∽

AFTERWORD

Mailing list: You can join my emailing list here : AnnamarieMorgan.com

Facebook page: AnnamarieMorganAuthor

You might also like to read the other books in the series:
Book 1: Death Master:
After months of mental and physical therapy, Yvonne Giles, an Oxford DI, is back at work and that's just how she likes it. So when she's asked to hunt the serial killer responsible for taking apart young women, the DI jumps at the chance but hides the fact she is suffering debilitating flashbacks. She is told to work with Tasha Phillips, an in-her-face, criminal psychologist. The DI is not enamoured with the idea. Tasha has a lot to prove. Yvonne has a lot to get over. A tentative link with a 20 year-old cold case brings them closer to the truth but events then take a horrifyingly personal turn.

Book 2: You Will Die

After apprehending an Oxford Serial Killer, and almost losing her life in the process, DI Yvonne Giles has left England for a quieter life in rural Wales.Her peace is shattered when she is asked to hunt a priest-killing psychopath, who taunts the police with messages inscribed on the corpses.Yvonne requests the help of Dr. Tasha Phillips, a psychologist and friend, to aid in the hunt. But the killer is one step ahead and the ultimatum, he sets them, could leave everyone devastated.

Book 3: Total Wipeout

A whole family is wiped out with a shotgun. At first glance, it's an open-and-shut case. The dad did it, then killed himself. The deaths follow at least two similar family wipeouts – attributed to the financial crash.

So why doesn't that sit right with Detective Inspector Yvonne Giles? And why has a rape occurred in the area, in the weeks preceding each family's demise? Her seniors do not believe there are questions to answer. DI Giles must therefore risk everything, in a high-stakes investigation ofa mysterious masonic ring and players in high finance.

Can she find the answers, before the next innocent family is wiped out?

Book 4: Deep Cut

In a tiny hamlet in North Wales, a female recruit is murdered whilst on Christmas home leave. Detective Inspector Yvonne Giles is asked to cut short her own leave, to investigate. Why was the young soldier killed? And is her death related to several alleged suicides at her army base? DI Giles this it is, and that someone powerful has a dark secret they will do anything to hide.

Book 5: The Pusher

Young men are turning up dead on the banks of the River Severn. Some of them have been missing for days or even weeks. The only thing the police can be sure of, is that the men have drowned. Rumours abound that a mythical serial killer has turned his attention from the Manchester canal to the waterways of Mid-Wales. And now one of CID's own is missing. A brand new recruit with everything to live for. DI Giles must find him before it's too late.

Book 6: Gone

Children are going missing. They are not heard from again until sinister requests for cryptocurrency go viral. The public must pay or the children die. For lead detective Yvonne Giles, the case is complicated enough. And then the unthinkable happens...

Book 7: Bone Dancer

A serial killer is murdering women, threading their bones back together, and leaving them for police to find. Detective Inspector Yvonne Giles must find him before more innocent victims die. Problem is, the killer wants her and will do anything he can to get her. Unaware that she, herself, is is a target, DI Giles risks everything to catch him.

Book 8: Blood Lost

A young man comes home to find his whole family missing. Half-eaten breakfasts and blood spatter on the lounge wall are the only clues to what happened...

Book 9: Angel of Death

He is watching. Biding his time. Preparing himself for a

torturous kill. Soaring above; lord of all. His journey, direct through the lives of the unsuspecting.

The Angel of Death is nigh.

The peace of the Mid-Wales countryside is shattered, when a female eco-warrior is found crucified in a public wood. At first, it would appear a simple case of finding which of the woman's enemies had had her killed. But DI Yvonne Giles has no idea how bad things are going to get. As the body count rises, she will need all of her instincts, and the skills of those closest to her, to stop the murderous rampage of the Angel of Death.

Book 10: Death in the Air

Several fatal air collisions have occurred within a few months in rural Wales. According to the local Air Accidents Investigation Branch (AAIB) inspector, it's a coincidence. Clusters happen. Except, this cluster is different. DI Yvonne Giles suspects it when she hears some of the witness statements but, when an AAIB inspector is found dead under a bridge, she knows it.

Something is way off. Yvonne is determined to get to the bottom of the mystery, but exactly how far down the treacherous rabbit hole is she prepared to go?

Book 11: Death in the Mist

The morning after a viscous sea-mist covers the seaside town of Aberystwyth, a young student lies brutalised within one hundred yards of the castle ruins.

DI Yvonne Giles' reputation precedes her. Having successfully captured more serial killers than some detectives have caught colds, she is seconded to head the murder investigation team, and hunt down the young woman's killer.

What she doesn't know, is this is only the beginning...

Book 12: Death under Hypnosis

When the secretive and mysterious Sheila Winters approaches Yvonne Giles and tells her that she murdered someone thirty years before, she has the DI's immediate attention.

Things get even more strange when Sheila states:

She doesn't know who.

She doesn't know where.

She doesn't know why.

Book 13: Fatal Turn

A seasoned hiker goes missing from the Dolfor Moors after recording a social media video describing a narrow cave he intends to explore. A tragic accident? Nothing to see here, until a team of cavers disappear on a coastal potholing expedition, setting off a string of events that has DI Giles tearing her hair out. What, or who is the thread that ties this series of disappearances together?

A serial killer, thriller murder-mystery set in Wales.

Remember to watch out for Book 15, coming soon...

Milton Keynes UK
Ingram Content Group UK Ltd.
UKHW022026041023
429950UK00010B/726